FROM SLEEP
UNBOUND

FROM SLEEP UNBOUND

Andrée Chedid

Translated from the French
Le Sommeil délivré
by Sharon Spencer

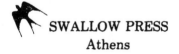 SWALLOW PRESS
Athens

© 1976 by Flammarion
English translation © 1983 by Sharon Spencer
Introduction © 1983, 1995 by Bettina Knapp

First Swallow Press/Ohio University Press edition printed 1983
Swallow Press/Ohio University Press
Athens, OH 45701

02 01   5 4 3 (pbk.)

Ohio University Press books
are printed on acid-free paper. ∞

Library of Congress Cataloging-in-Publication Data

Chedid, Andrée.
        From sleep unbound.

        "Translated from the original French title Le Sommeil délivré."
        ISBN 0-8040-0837-X(pbk.)
        I. Title.
        PQ2605.H4245S613   1983   843'.914   82-22459
                                                    CIP

to Louis,

this first novel

Woman may be compared to a very deep
body of water; one can never
predict the power of the undertow.

Vizir Ptahhotep,
"Instruction on the Subject of Women,"
Egypt, about 2600 B.C.

Foreword

Poet, dramatist, essayist, novelist, wife, mother, grand-mother—Andrée Chedid is one of France's outstanding literary figures. Her way is profound and sensitive, her vision innovative in its archetypal delineations, her aesthetic is lyrical, dense, symbolistic—a blend of the real and the unreal, the Occident and the Middle East. The protagonists of her novels emerge from a universal mold; they are eternal in their philosophical and psychological configurations—they have stepped into life full-blown from the dream.

Andrée Chedid, who is of Egypto-Lebanese origin, was born in Cairo in 1920. She received her B.A. degree from the American University in her native city. Married at the age of 21 to Louis Chedid, a medical student, Andrée Chedid spent the next two years (1942–45) in Lebanon. The couple moved to Paris in 1946 where Louis Chedid earned his degree in medicine, then became associated with the Institut Pasteur. The Chedids have two children and six grandchildren.

Andrée Chedid has repeatedly said that she is the product of two civilizations, two ways of life, and two psyches. These dichotomies, however, are fused in the works of art which are her writings—stilled in giant frescoes, visualizations and dramatizations replete with mysterious and arcane forces, spheres bathed in subliminal darkness, insalubrious realms, as well as crisp, stark luminosities which crystallize sensations, revealing the most imperceptible of sublime feelings. Unlike the New Wave novelists, such as Michel Butor or Alain Robbe-Grillet, who consider the novel to be a type of puzzle, a mythology difficult to unravel, whose works are divested of plot and characters and whose beings are perpetually following repetitive patterns; or the writings of Nathalie Sarraute, whose dramas stem directly from the interplay of tropisms, which is what she calls those inner movements, those sensations and hidden forces within each individual that are at the root of gestures, words, and feelings; or of Françoise-Mallet Joris' dynamic clusters whose *raison d'être* focuses on questions of appearance and reality set not in any philosophical or political terms, but as part of a theological climate based on hope. Chedid's novels resemble to a certain degree, Marguerite Duras' works such as *The Ravishing of Lol V. Stein* or *The Vice-Consul,* sequences of essences flowing onto the stage in evanescent forms and shapes, capturing the fleeting, enclosing ephemeral thoughts and feelings in dazzling poetic images.

Andrée Chedid's childhood days and her early memories, particularly those associated with Egypt, play an important role in her formation as a writer. Emotions and images, as stamped in her writings, bear the impress of a dry and parched land with its sun-drenched tonalities ranging from deep ochre to a sandy-brown glare, from seemingly endless skies, depicted in nuanced tones of incandescent blues, set against a blazing sun and the sleepy, sometimes turbid waters of the Nile. Her novels are bathed in endlessly shifting emotional climates, disclosing and secreting shapes and hues, energy patterns transmuted into human beings or into landscapes—impenetrable domains where purity cohabits with depravity. As Andrée Chedid wrote in an interview:

> ... as far as I am concerned, it is less a matter of nostalgic return to the past, of a concerted search for memories, than it is a need to experience the permanent presence of an inner sentiment— pulsations, movements, chants, misery and joy, sun and serenity, which are inherent to the Middle East. I seem to feel all these emotions pulsating within me. I believe I was very much marked

by both the poverty and the benevolence of those around me. I felt compelled to speak of the simple people in my novels because they seem to be closer to the essentials in life, to the elementary aspects of nature. Of love, death, and of life.

Andrée Chedid's writings are many and varied. They include such novels as *From Sleep Unbound* (*Le Sommeil délivré*, 1952), *The Sixth Day* (*Le Sixième jour*, 1960), *The Other* (*L'Autre*, 1969), *The Fertile City* (*La Cité fertile*, 1972), *Nefertiti and Akhenaton's Dream* (*Nefertiti et le rêve d'Akhnaton*, 1974), *Les Marches de sable* (*Steps in the Sand*, 1981), *La Femme de Job* (*Job's Wife*, 1993); collections of poems entitled *Primal Face* (*Visage premier*, 1972), *Texts for a Countenance* (*Textes pour une figure*, 1949), *Caverns and Suns* (*Cavernes et soleils*, 1979); successfully produced plays, *Bérénice of Egypt* (*Bérénice d'Egypte*, 1968), *Numbers* (*Les Nombres*, 1968). *The Showman* (*Le Montreur*, 1969); essays on Lebanon, war, poetics, the art of writing. She is the recipient of many awards, among them, the Louise Labé prize for poetry (1976), and the Goncourt prize for short story (1979).

Both the Occident and the Middle East are always present in her novels. Universal needs and feelings are stamped with collective as well as individual yearnings—set apart or opposed to environment or family situations—or themselves. The tension provoked by the innervating sensations which flow forth are evoked in muffled and muted tones, feeding and dilating the images implicit in her works.

Peoples and civilizations fascinate Andrée Chedid. As such, past is ushered into existence, creatures are enticed to spin their webs, to evolve, to act, while revealing both blemished and unblemished inner worlds. Her novels may be looked upon as meeting places between author and the creatures of her fantasy—and the reader—enriching one another deeply and permanently. The dialogue fostered in this tripartite dynamic arouses suspense, but most of all, fleshes out *feeling*.

Andrée Chedid's novels are based on myths, that is, impersonal experiences. Past, present, and future fuse into an eternal present, grow, paradoxically, into a single harmony and/or cacophony. A theme may stem from a kind of anecdote, as it does in *The Other,* then expand in dimension, revealing the inner workings of a death/rebirth ritual. An old man is determined—and this despite all odds—to save the life of a young man, a foreigner, who had, it was thought, been the victim of an earthquake. He is convinced that the young man is alive beneath the rubble. Obdurate, the peasant pursues his arduous search into the profound recesses of the earth. Mythically, we see a man's progressive and willed emergence from obscurity, his terrible struggle against the forces of darkness—his faith in life, in the individual. The old man's simple and earthy vocabulary, and the passion with which he imbues his task, allow him to pass from the shadow world of unknown subliminal forces beneath the earth, to the sunlit sphere of enlightenment. From One world to *The Other*—death to life, action born of desire!

Language for Andrée Chedid is an instrument which allows her to decant her feelings, concretize her thoughts, philosophical and aesthetic views. Set in single and multiple sequences of energetic patterns, rhythmic groupings, and lyrical sonorities, her novels resound with subtle blendings, capture and encapsulate the reader in their flow. A voice always presides in each of her works: disconcertingly at times, assuagingly at other moments, it expresses the pain, anguish, joy, and the sensuality which exist inchoate in the mysterious sub-climates of a soul. This voice, which emanates from the very depths of being, links past, present, and future in ductile essences and sensations. The voice is attached to the land; it speaks mightily of Egypt, Lebanon, and France—elements of each, undefined and undelimited in an endless potent vision. The voice inhabiting Andrée Chedid's novels transcends geographical boundaries; it bears the stamp of universality.

The voice which emerges from her works is linked and nurtured by the spiritual, psychological, and visceral configurations of her characters. Solitary, they frequently walk their own dismal paths, a prey to fantasies, terrors not always of their own making, but due in part to social stigmas imposed upon them by centuries of social conventions. Such beings yearn to be understood, to communicate their longings, to breach distances, pierce through matter and bathe in a wall-less world, warmed by a feeling sun rather than by the icy climes of a world engulfed in blackness. Strong and virile women also figure in Chedid's novels, positive mother principles who know how to handle their pained lives, to assuage torment, assume helpful stances during agonizing moments.

Unlike the characters or non-characters of Butor, Robbe-Grillet, Sarraute, and Claude Simon, Chedid's creatures are not literary equivalents of people she has known or not known. They do not fit into a system or classification; they cannot be forced bodily into an opus, squarely or mathematically placed here and there. Her beings are amalgams or blendings—alloys in the alchemical sense—of memories and phantasms. They are never limited by area or intellectual stratifications. They are fluid forms emerging from a subliminal world, alive, breathing, acting and reacting to forces outside of their control or those over which they may have some authority. Although Andrée Chedid maintains that the people inhabiting her novels do not resemble her in any way, her protagonists bear the stamp of her personality—wistful, poetic, sensitive, compassionate, understanding—yet, they are also merciless and cruel if too acutely pressed, if pain grows unbearable; fulguratingly explosive situations are of their making. It is this very *livingness,* this poetic quality of fusing emotion and feeling with the workaday world, revealed in muted, subdued, and controlled overtones, which makes her works unique.

Nature is also a living entity in Andrée Chedid's novels— a heaving, pulsating body. In *The Fertile City,* for example, the various forms delineating this metropolis are expressed in terms of blocks of images, evanescent in texture. Primary colors emerge in a series of stark blendings; metals take on emotional tonalities, they burn with force as if exposed to intense heat and great passion, then flow through intricate verbal patterns; elements, such as earth, water, and air, are transformed by the wizardry of Chedid's pen into rows of concrete houses, vast landscapes, clumps of bushy trees. The city is the backdrop for the situations enacted in *The Fertile City.* Alefa, the archetypal mother, could be a hundred or a thousand years old—she is ageless. A dancer, she practices one of the most ancient arts known, one of the most elemental forms of expression. Alefa, however, is no ordinary entertainer. Both human and non-human, when she walks she "oscillates," and in so doing, manipulates her limbs, concretizes her throughts and emotions in sequences of hieratic gestures which seem to float through space. Natural forces such as the tree, the stone, a tear, even silence and air come to life under Chedid's verbal baton. A positive mother figure, Alefa nourishes, encourages, yields her embrace and comfort to those in need of warmth and understanding. Against this extraordinary mythical personification, are enacted the petty worries, jealousies, rancors, and loves of the protagonists.

Andrée Chedid's characters are ambivalent. Rooted and uprooted, their joys and pains are woven into living and palpable forces which capture, hold, then release their loves and hates in spiritual, subliminal and phenomenological spheres. There they dwell, along with multiple fantasy figures, each attracting and repelling those within their reach. Living in an atemporal time scheme, having rejected overly limited or specific personality traits, Chedid's beings are people "of all season." Archetypal, they are *molded* from universal and eternal fabric.

In *Nefertiti and Akhenaton's Dream*, the queen is mother, wife, woman of insight and strength; she is the filament that binds, links, and fosters events and feelings. Plunged into what seems to be a timeless era—1375–1358 B.C.—the reader experiences a cyclical rather than eschatological time scheme. He participates as a dynamic entity in a world offering multiple possibilities and opportunities. Many of Chedid's novels center around women, and *Nefertiti and Akhenaton's Dream* is no exception. She excels in depicting their needs, desires, longings, and sorrows. She understands their many faces, their layerings, their mysteries. As such, the feminine principle in *Nefertiti and Akhenaton's Dream* is depicted in rhythmic patterns, harmonies, dissonances, prolonged silences which reverberate in cadencelike fashion throughout the novel, supporting its plot and characterizations, and underscoring its inner tensions. Colors are also fleshed out in haunting, provoking and traumatic hues from

bronzed yellow to deep turquoise, thus setting affective rela-
tionships; moods based on palettes, color supplements. Chedid's hand is sure and certain when it comes to architectural
descriptions: Egyptian temples, palaces, inner chambers,
pyramids, stand high and mighty in the distance, like stark
but flamboyant mural paintings or sculptures, carvings set
on ancient temples and sarcophogi. They capture in words
the immobility, elegance, remoteness of those powerful mon-
archs of old.

In *From Sleep Unbound,* so exquisitely translated by
Sharon Spencer, we are introduced to a family of characters
who, like Giacometi statues, are stripped of unnecessary
accessories, both visually and verbally. As they move about,
weaving intricate forms in space, they, too, bear the imprint
of ancient frescoes dimmed with the patina of age. The stati-
cally-paced dialogue injects a sense of timelessness and
atemporality into events and into personalities, capturing
the stillness and terror of eternity. Yet an urgency, extreme
and traumatic, also emerges powerfully in *From Sleep Unbound.* Indeed, the novel begins with a crisis, as do the
Racinian tragedies, a crushing impact. Compressed feelings
are unleashed at the very outset.

From Sleep Unbound generates excitement not by exaggerated rhythmic effects or plot lines, but rather by the
juxtaposition of tempi, feelings, yearnings, and longings.
Samya, the paralyzed wife of Boutros, is depicted as a deeply
introverted being, her needs held at bay throughout the
novel until the conflagration which tears down the world of
solitude. Her paralysis, symbolically viewed, is a manifesta-
tion of her inability to cope with daily existence, the routine
of life—her rejection of her pariah state, of her excruciating
pain. She cannot walk; helpless, divested of a life attitude,
she is cut off from earth, from all human company. Only her
inner world is subsumed: that subliminal region where
moods and anguishes are viewed as fluid and opalescent
entities, where terror heightens feelings of apprehension;
foreboding is spun into the very fabric of the novel in
premonitory images of apocalyptic power.

From Sleep Unbound takes its readers directly into the
heart of the woman's world. Samya is the product of a con-

temporary middle-Eastern upbringing with its harsh and brutal customs, particularly concerning women, whose earthly existences serve certain specific purposes: to serve man and to bear children. Her husband, unfeeling, detached, uninterested, does not even notice the beauty which radiates from her face: large brown eyes, smooth olive skin, jet black hair, slim features. Daily, Samya feels her life eroding, slowly crumbling, slipping, dematerializing into oblivion. Sensations of uselessness reduce her to a state of psychological penury, of fragmentation. Then, anger and resentment, even hatred intrude, resulting perhaps out of sheer dismay at her own passivity. Her sister-in-law, Rachida, whom her husband depends upon so implicitly and explicitly to run the cotton farm, arrives. Rancor swells. Jealousy. As Samya pursues her story, defoliating her feelings, exposing her fulgurating pain like a raw nerve, images are marked with burnt umber, gray, black, darkened configurations. The atmosphere is suffused with feelings swelling with rapture and sensuality, also with bouts of rage and outrage.

Samya's psyche is the prototype of the Arab woman—enslaved by her husband and by society. Misunderstood, subservient to her husband's needs, Samya lives in her own muted realm—a world of whispers, fleeting emotions, expressed in a closed walled-in world of murmurs and half-tints—fear. To reveal the inner workings of *From Sleep Unbound* would be to divulge a secret domain, arcana as spun into the ritual of life by the cryptic hand of the writer-artist that Andrée Chedid is.

From Sleep Unbound captures not one woman's world, but that of *all* women, whether they lived cloistered and closeted in a society bound by retrograde customs or in a modern metropolis, liberated for all intents and purposes, but imprisoned within their own psychological cells. *From Sleep Unbound* is a concerted probing, a poetic search for a "direct breath," an eternal voice, a single dream, participating in the cosmic flow; catalyzed by an ever-searching soul.

BETTINA L. KNAPP

Hunter College
and the Graduate Center, CUNY

Translator's Preface

This translation of Andrée Chedid's novel *Le Sommeil délivré* is based partly upon a literal rendering of the work from French to English by Roselyne Eddé. I am very grateful for the existence of this earlier text, for it facilitated my own work by providing a very useful foundation on which I was able to build a more literary version of the novel.

Le Sommeil délivré depends for its poetic artistry upon certain rhythmical patterns which are composed into a music for the ear. The original French is incantatory and obsessive, as befits Chedid's subject and her protagonist's situation. Throughout, I have attempted either to preserve or to simulate the rhythms of the original creation as well as the equally important classical and timeless nature of the novel's elegantly simple language and imagery. The most difficult problem was to select for the title a phrase which would suggest the complexity of *Le Sommeil délivré*, which alludes not only to awakening and to release, to the sudden liberation in action of accumulated rage and resentment, but also to the crucial "deliverance" of the birth process. "From sleep unbound" suggests the essence of Samya's definitive action at the same time that it emphasizes the novel's unifying metaphor, that of sleep.

I undertook the translation of *Le Sommeil délivré* in a

spirit of admiration for this book which now offers English language readers an intimate view into the soul of a woman whose life is its own tragic comment and whose ultimate destiny is oddly satisfying when one considers the brutal conditions she was compelled to experience as her life.

If these words seem enigmatic, they are soon to find explanation in the pages that follow.

Part One

The rays of the sun were already less blinding as they fell on the walls of the white house. In the distance an arm of the Nile stretched toward the suppleness of a shadow.

1 Rachida came outside to breathe the freshness and, just as she did every evening, she rested her body against the grayish white wall, waiting for her brother to return. Her bun of gray hair and her drab garments always bore flecks of plaster.

Her brother's name was Boutros. He supervised the farming of the surrounding lands that belonged to a wealthy man who preferred to live in the city. Three times a year this man, the owner, came to collect the money due him from the rents paid by the fellahin. For these rare visits he had built a stone house for himself. It stood facing the smaller house; its shutters were always closed.

Boutros appeared at the end of the narrow road. Above his face, which seemed to be squeezed tightly between his shoulders, rose his cylinder-shaped fez.

The double wooden door stood open. The brother and sister exchanged greetings, he moving on into the house. Turning, Rachida followed his figure with her eyes as Boutros climbed the first hollowed-out steps. There came a bend in the stairway and then she could no longer hear the sound of his steps. The storeroom in which the cotton was kept was on the floor above. Rachida listened to the squeaking of the doorknob as

Boutros turned it, assuring himself, as he did every evening, that it was locked. The office was located on the same floor. Rachida listened to the sound of the key in the lock, of the door opening. In this way she accompanied her brother on his evening rounds; she knew his movements so well.

Now he was entering the office. The walls and ceilings were covered with flaking plaster that sometimes fell onto the shoulders of the accountant, crumbling down the front of his jacket. Frowning, Boutros would be opening the drawers, peeling off a sheet from the calendar, approaching the large black safe. Rachida could see it all as if she were there. She also saw the huge portrait of a man wearing a fez and a neatly trimmed moustache, a man seated in a dignified posture; he was the man who had created this great fortune in land. Between his legs there stood a cane with a gold handle on which he rested his hands. He resembled the present landowner, who was, in fact, his grandson. When Boutros passed this portrait he always bowed slightly.

The visit to the office was completed now and Boutros began to walk back toward the stairway. Rachida listened as his steps began to grow heavier, for he was moving toward the three rooms on the third floor. It was here that he lived with Rachida and Samya, his wife, the cripple. Helpless in spite of her youth!

What if Rachida should catch a disease like that! This Samya attracted disasters. Her two legs immobilized. For what sin was God punishing her?

Now Rachida couldn't hear anything. Boutros had entered the large foyer and Rachida told herself that she had earned the right to go for her evening walk.

She passed by the two houses, the one that she had just left, dull, streaked with gray; the other belonging to the absent landlord freshly repainted, the shutters closed. As she walked through the dust Rachida looked down at the darned toes of her stockings that poked through the openings in her slippers.

The narrow road led to a large enclosure, abandoned at this time of day, where the fellahin threshed the corn. She often lingered here for a breath of air before the evening meal. But not this evening. A calf had been born during the night. She would go to the cow shed to admire him.

She needed new slippers, new stockings as well. With their
robes down to their ankles and their bare feet, the fellahin
had nothing to worry about. But she couldn't go about as
they did; she had to maintain her rank by keeping her distance. Rachida was careful about this. Unlike her sister-in-
law, that Samya, who had no pride. Before she became
paralyzed, Samya had wanted to pass her time in only one
way, wandering about the village, mingling with just anyone. Samya claimed that she was happy doing this. Boutros
had reprimanded her many times.

It was the close of a day like all other days. Rachida
walked toward the cow shed. Around her head she wore a
kerchief edged with small red plush balls.

It was the close of a day like all other days, except that the
sun was a little less intense than usual. There was the bleat-
ing of a sheep, the barking of a dog, the fluttering of pigeons'
wings.

The end of an afternoon like other afternoons. Rachida
could foresee nothing.

She will tell everything, Rachida promises herself. She
will tell everything. People have evil thoughts sometimes.
She will know how to silence venomous tongues. She will tell
everything; she has nothing to hide.

This is the way it was. She was walking down the road. She
was going to the cowshed to visit the baby calf. Boutros, her
brother, had greeted her as was his habit before entering the
house and climbing the stairs. She had listened to his footsteps until he had passed through the door that opened onto
the foyer of their three rooms. Everything as usual. After
that she had heard nothing at all.

The shed was not far off. A shaky structure held up by
half-rotted wooden boards with sackcloth partitions tacked
into the boards to separate the animals from one another in
makeshift stalls.

As Rachida approached, Zeinab came out carrying a child
on one shoulder and a bucket of milk in her free hand. She
was too busy to notice Rachida. But everyone on the farm
knew that Rachida took a walk at the same hour every
evening.

Who would even dream of reproaching her? The atmosphere of their three rooms was so confined; she needed to

get away for a breath of air. She was not a demanding woman. Ever since she had come here two years earlier, she had not even gone as far away as the town. Rachida did not need entertainment; she was utterly devoted to her brother. But taking the air was different; it was a matter of health. One invalid in the house was enough!

The cowshed was dark, but Rachida knew every corner and she found the new calf at once. Frail legs, silky brown hair, a huge soft tongue with which he kept licking his nose. Repeatedly, Rachida stroked him, murmuring into his ear, pushing his head against her black apron.

Rachida lingered. She knew the names of each of the animals; she herself had chosen the mare's name. Picking up two nails that had fallen onto the earthen floor, she looked about, searching for a piece of wood which she could use as a hammer to replace them. But the nails were rusty and crooked, and she had difficulty driving them back into the posts. She hammered and hammered until she thought she would deafen herself.

Maybe that was the moment when it happened.

She will tell everything, Rachida vows. Everything that she had done from the moment Boutros had disappeared around the bend in the stairway. All of that, and everything else as well.

The damp straw in the shed stuck to the soles of her slippers. The mangers were mostly deserted, the fodder scattered about the earth. Ammal had not yet returned with her sheep; she was the granddaughter of the shepherd, Abou Mansour.

That Ammal was good for nothing! Rachida had seen the softness with which Ammal treated the cripple. Sniveling over her each time she carried up the cheese. Ammal said that Samya was too good to suffer. Too good!

Still complaining to herself, Rachida began to walk back toward the house. At the entrance, she took off her slippers and rubbed them together to shake off the mud. On the other side of the road the fields stretched out as far as the eye could see, flat and green, crisscrossed by paths of black sand. Set back from the village, a clutter of muddy buildings behind a thin veil of trees, stood the two houses, face to face.

Rachida put her slippers back on, noting how they had faded. As she entered the house, she thought about those other slippers underneath the shawl that covered Samya's useless legs. They were black and lustrous. What good were they? Why not suggest an exchange of slippers with the cripple? But if she did this Rachida would have to deal, as always, with Samya's selfishness. As she moved toward the stairway, Rachida recounted her woes.

Without hurrying she climbed the stairs. When she reached the door of the storeroom and that of the office she stopped and examined the locks with a sharp eye. This was her way of helping her brother. But everything was in order; Boutros never overlooked anything.

If only she had known! If only she had been able to guess! She wouldn't have bothered with locks and doors. She would have rushed upstairs. She would have awakened the entire village!

It was a day just like all other days. She could not have foreseen anything.

The bannister with its wrought iron flowers was shaky; you didn't dare lean on it. The stairs were concave, worn by generations of footsteps. The solitary window had lost its panes of glass.

On the third floor the door to the foyer was standing open. Boutros knew that his sister would not be gone long. As he did every evening, he had placed his cane in the copper stand. The hat rack was empty. Boutros never took off his fez until he came to the table for the evening meal. A somber velvet tapestry separated the foyer from the room in which the cripple lay during the days, a room that also served as the dining room. The drapes were always closed; Samya could not bear the slightest ray of light.

Because of her devotion to her brother, Rachida never left the house before evening. The women of the village brought her eggs, milk, meat, and various vegetables. They would arrive, their arms full, their black robes brushing against the white walls, and they would laugh through the folds of their veils, now and then pulling them over their faces. Nostrils quivering slightly, they would laugh and their hesitant merriment would ring out as their eyes moved about the room as swiftly as mice scurrying into their corners. They might say: "There are new chairs in the house of the overseer." Or, "This evening in the house of the Nazer they will eat stuffed eggplant."

When the women left, Rachida would take up her work again; she preferred to do everything herself. Whenever anyone else was around, the cripple would manage silently to call attention to herself.

Friday was the day of prayers and on this day Boutros went neither to the fields nor to the office. The holiness of the day did not concern him as he was a Christian, but he observed the customs of his fellow Moslems. "I am a believer," he would say whenever he talked of his own religion, and he was proud of the fact that his sister Rachida never missed mass on Sunday. "As for myself, work sometimes prevents me from going. But I believe that God will forgive me."

All week long Rachida waited for Friday.

She would prepare the meal in two copper pots. Toward noon at Boutros's call, she would come downstairs and together they would walk toward the banks of the canal. Rachida would place the pots one on top of the other, wrap them up in a white towel, knot the ends and pick them up. The pots were heavy, weighing down her shoulders, and she would pant, changing her burden from one hand to the other as she hurried to keep up with her brother. He always walked ahead of her, drawing circles in the air with his bamboo cane. Sometimes he would take off his fez and mop the sweat from his forehead with his handkerchief.

How well they suited one another, the two of them! They would have their meal together under the weeping willow trees, whose branches swooped down into the water, protecting you from the sun by enclosing you in a cradle of greenery.

Boutros would be unusually talkative. Rachida would nod in agreement. Then Rachida would talk and Boutros would say:

"You are an excellent woman!"

"You are a saint!"

"It is good that I brought you here."

"What would have become of me?"

How well they suited one another, the two of them! The cripple never came outdoors with them. A wheelchair would have been a waste of money. What for? They were happier this way, without her.

But if she had known! If Rachida had known, if she had been able to foresee it! She would never have left the cripple's side. She would have bought the chair with her own money. She would have wheeled Samya in front of herself always, without taking her eyes off her for a second. She would have pulled the wheelchair with her everywhere, into the kitchen, out onto the balcony. She would have asked for help to carry it up and down the stairs. She would have taken Samya for excursions into the road, to the cowshed, into the barn, along the river banks and over the smooth green paths. At the risk of exhaustion, she would have dragged the cripple with her everywhere, always!

On that particular day Rachida had hesitated before entering the room in which her sister-in-law lay. There were fava beans on the fire. Were they cooked yet? She opened the door to the kitchen. The burner was roaring with a strong blue flame. She raised the cover of the pot, plunged a fork into the beans. No, they were not quite done.

In the entrance hall everything was in place: the chair, the copper stand, the hat rack with its mirror, the threadbare velvet draperies. Samya would have liked a thin cotton hanging; she said that the touch of the velvet on her hands made her shiver!

Rachida shrugged. The eccentricities of a hysteric!

With two hands she seized the velvet drapes and pulled them apart. Then she thrust her head forward so that she could see better into the shadows.

* * *

The worn soles of her blue felt slippers made a dull thudding sound on the floor as she rushed to the shutters which she opened with a clatter, then to the cement balcony and finally to the iron balustrade.

"Help! Help! Come quickly! Quickly! Help!" Rachida
grasped the railing and thrust her body forward as she
screamed. Her skirt jerked up over her bony shins, exposing
the crude darned spots in her cotton stockings. Her head
trembled so violently that long pins slipped out of her bun
of gray hair. From the wall opposite, her voice ricocheted
back to her, distorted: "Help!"

It seemed as though the force of her cries might sweep her
to the ground below. She did not see anything. She stood
with her back to the room, her back turned toward that
other woman. She looked straight ahead. She screamed:

"Someone has killed him! Someone has killed him! Come,
come, all of you! Someone has killed the Nazer!"

Names came into her memory. She called them out in any
order, without thinking:

"Hussein! Khaled! Abou Mansour! Help! Someone has
killed my brother!"

She did not want to turn around. Above all, she did not
want to turn around. Behind her was that woman, that
Samya, and her stare was piercing Rachida's back. Above
all, she did not want to turn around until the others arrived.
When would they come! When would they all come! When
would they fill up the room! She called out, concentrating on
the sound of her voice:

"Barsoum! Farid! Fatma, you Fatma! Where are you?
Someone has killed the Nazer! My brother is dead! Hurry!"

Her voice, imprisoned in the alley which separated the
two houses, ricocheted from one to the other, but it did not
reach the fields nor the village, buried under a shroud of
dust. Her voice crashed against the walls. It rose higher,
seeking to overcome the distance and to penetrate the fields
and the village.

"Come! Come! Everyone come!" cried the voice.

The railing of the balcony cut into Rachida's palms. Her
hair straggled down her neck. She did not want to turn
around, to see Boutros's fallen body, to meet the stare of that
motionless woman.

She wanted to forget everything. Oh, if only they would
come quickly! To forget everything, until they finally came!

To be nothing more than this cry:
"Help! Avenge us!"

* * *

Nearly hidden in her armchair, the woman said nothing.
The shutters were open; the light flowed everywhere. She
was no longer used to it; she was blinking. A faded shawl
concealed her legs.

Rachida cried in strange tones that clashed against one
another. The woman's pale hands rested on the arms of her
chair. Her elbows were slightly raised as if she were getting
ready to stand up. Her dark hair gleamed; her ears were
partly concealed by a violet band. Pinned to her unbleached
muslin blouse was a safety pin adorned with a blue stone,
like a brooch. A necklace of square green beads was loosely
knotted around her throat.

The dead man's head was resting on her feet. She did not
seem to feel its weight.

Rachida screamed and leaned even further over the railing of the balcony, revealing her bony shins and darned
stockings. Why was she in such a condition? She was in
danger of toppling off the balcony.

One day Boutros had killed a crow with a single shot. He
had been so pleased to see the bird fall out of the top of the
tree! In the sunlight the crow was black, tinged with grayish
light and blood-stained. Remembering this made her feel
anxious. If she were to tumble into the alley between the
houses, she would be black and gray, with blood on her skirt
and her hair disheveled.

The other woman was far away. All of this seemed like a
tale that one might hear while standing on the railway platform waiting for the train to leave. A story from some distant place.

Rachida screamed. She screamed. Her voice was becoming
hoarse. She shook her head; she looked straight ahead. Not
once did she turn around.

If Boutros had been there, if he were not already icy, he
would have come to his sister's side. Without hesitating,

he would have come to her. He would have gotten up and joined her on the balcony, and they would have stood together with their shoulders touching. They were almost the same height. The two of them would have leaned over together above the balustrade. They would have cried out with one voice.

After a while Boutros would have turned around. He would have asked Rachida to be quiet and he would have turned to face Samya.

He would have taken several steps forward, then, with his arms crossed, he would have looked inside the room, into the armchair and beneath the violet headband. If he had not already been cold, he would have been there facing Samya, harsh, implacable, shaking his head as if scolding a child.

Then he would have returned to the balcony to his sister's side. Their voices would have risen together again.

This is what he would have done if he had been there with his face animated under the red cap. Now the fez lay in the center of the room, abandoned to the last rays of the sun.

Later, Boutros would have said:

"Did she have anything to worry about? She had everything. It was my sister who was wearing herself out. Did I ever deprive her of anything? Was I unfaithful to her? She had everything!"

These would have been his words if he had been able to stand on his stiffening feet.

"She had everything! A husband, a home, good food! What more could a woman want? I have known for a long time that she would come to a bad end. My religion prevented me from denouncing her. Now I can do nothing more for her! Take her! Do whatever you want with her!"

Motionless, the high back of her chair rising above her head, the woman would have gone right on killing herself.

Today as yesterday, she would have continued to wear herself out until she succeeded in killing herself.

Light was flowing into the corners of the room, catching the flecks of dust, gathering upon the artificial flowers in the earthenware vase. They could live without water, these immortal flowers, rustling like dry leaves when anyone accidentally brushed them in passing. The two green leather chairs were waiting for no one. A halo of sunlight encircled the fez.

Still clinging to the balcony railing, Rachida went on screaming. Everyone seemed to have grown used to her cries.

The mirror gave to each object wrested from the shadows an image both realistic and cruel. The woman saw nothing but these objects. She did not look at herself, nor did she look any longer at the red stain on the chest of the dead man.

* * *

Since dawn she had known that Boutros would be lying in this way in this exact place. After that she had thought no more about it. Between her boredom and the comings and goings of Rachida, the woman had passed this day as she passed all the others. No sooner had Rachida left one corner of the room than she reappeared in another, her lips moving endlessly. When she disappeared into the adjacent room, her grumbling seeped in under the doorsill. Countering the incessant disturbance of Rachida's motions, the semi-darkness gave the other woman an opportunity to close her eyes for a while and to forget everything.

It was around six o'clock when Rachida went down for her evening walk. Soon after this Boutros would come upstairs. The woman always waited for him. Because of the closed shutters, she was surrounded by darkness, and she sat tensely in the dark, lying in wait for his footsteps.

She heard him cross the threshold and she raised herself a little in order to hear better. The various objects were barely visible in the half-light of the room. The woman was attentive only to his steps, deliberate and heavy. She counted them step after step as they rose toward the slightly open door.

His face tense, she envisioned Boutros stopping at the door of the storeroom, stopping at the door of the office, his manner suspicious as he tested the keys in the locks. She easily envisioned the manner in which he crossed the landing before entering the foyer. Then the harsh sound of his cane when he dropped it into the umbrella stand.

Boutros never loitered.

She felt a current of air brush the back of her neck, and she knew that he had opened the velvet draperies. His steps entered the room. Soon Boutros would stand before her and he would embrace her, kiss her. This time she knew that it would be too much to bear.

Since dawn when she was placed in her armchair, she had been hiding the gun. Most of the time Boutros carried it in the right pocket of his jacket. He often said: "It is necessary to carry a gun. You never can tell. . . ." But sometimes he left it in the chest of drawers between his shirts.

At first Samya had thought of it as a dangerous object. Then one evening, while her husband and Rachida stood talking on the balcony, she had opened the drawer near her bed, removed the revolver and laid it on the sheet. She had turned it over and over in her hands until its feel became familiar. She had tested the trigger with her finger. Then she had replaced the revolver in the drawer. Rachida and Boutros were always talking together on the balcony. They spoke in such low tones that she was unable to hear what they said. She had slipped the gun back between the shirts. The woman was not yet thinking of using it.

Why this particular day? The night had not been disturbing. Still, it was on this particular morning that she had decided to end everything. She knew that she would use the gun. Boutros would bend over her, his arms dangling, offering his lips. He would be wearing his fez tilted toward the back, exposing his forehead on which a few drops of sweat always glistened. His lips would approach, huge and brown, filled with saliva at the corners. He would bend over her. She would see nothing but his lips and his scarlet fez. This would be unbearable. He would stoop over her once more. He would stoop over her one more time.

*   *   *

He would never get up again.

The shot had gone off so close to his chest that the noise had been muffled.

The man had lost his balance, his arms waving about grasping for support. He had fallen forward and the fez had tumbled off his head and rolled into the middle of the room like an empty flowerpot.

Samya had fired again.

The man seemed drunk. He mumbled indistinct words. He staggered, then reeled, bringing his hands to his forehead as he fell onto his knees.

The woman had loosened her grip and the gun slid from her hands, making a thud on the floor.

She looked away; she longed to be far away. She yearned to abandon her own body, to leave it to whomever came along, and to think about something else. For the first time she had performed, accomplished, completed an action, and now it was necessary to separate herself from it. Later, there would be time to dream about it. The others would see to that.

The man's head seemed to become heavy. She bent toward the chest in which life was still struggling. Then, as if all the threads snapped at the same instant, Boutros collapsed against her legs.

*   *   *

The dead man's head was not heavy.

The woman breathed more easily. She detached herself from her action; she did not concern herself with it any longer. In order to see the dead man's head she had to support herself by clasping the arms of her chair while she leaned forward. And what would he then awaken in her? Perhaps nothing at all.

At this moment she thought that she might be able to stand up; her legs would obey her, she felt sure. But where could she go? It was too late; nothing ever begins over again. Buried in her armchair, right now she was farther away from this place than she would ever be able to walk. A weight had fallen from her chest, carrying with it the room itself and this very moment. This story was no longer her story.

Soon the house would be filled with the sounds of Rachida's return. She would cross the threshold; one would be able to hear her climbing the stairs. In spite of her sixty years, Rachida climbed quickly. She often boasted about what strong legs she had, stating and restating her belief that one never grew old if one had nothing bad on one's conscience.

Just as she did every evening, Rachida would test all the locks with her heavily veined hands. As suspicious as her brother, she would examine every single door. They had duplicates of all the keys. She would climb the stairs without even leaning on the shaky bannister. The door to the foyer was partly open, she would push against it.

Rachida was hesitating before the velvet draperies, the ones that she refused to replace. She insisted that velvet was "rich looking." She said that in the white house opposite their house, in the landlord's house, all the curtains were velvet, as well as the armchairs and the sofas.

One would be able to hear her moving into the kitchen before the roar of the lighted stove would muffle the sound of her steps. She would return, grumbling: "I really go to too much trouble! No one helps me. At my age, to have to wait on a woman who could be my daughter! I do it all for Boutros, may God bless him! What would become of him without me?"

As soon as Boutros arrived, she made a fuss over him. After dinner they would pull their chairs close together and they would whisper:

"We're talking quietly so we won't wear you out."

"In your condition," they said.

*   *   *

Soon, Rachida would open the velvet drapes and she would run across the room. She would throw open the shutters, allowing the light to pour into the room. She would lean over the balcony and she would begin to scream.

All of this no longer mattered. Bubbles bursting above the water, that was all.

* * *

Rachida screamed but no one heard her!

In the village the women were entirely taken up with their children. They were tending to the little ones and they had ears for no one else. They were giving orders in order to make themselves feel important before their husbands came in from the fields.

"Ahmed, come here. Your father will soon come back home."

"Saïd, go and bring me water."

"Tahia? Where is Tahia?"

"Amin, put down those pebbles. You know your father likes to find you here when he returns."

"May your soul be damned, Tahia! Next year you'll see! I'll send you off to the fields!"

Rachida would have to go on waiting; soon her voice would be little more than a murmur. Night would fall, and she would still be here, clinging to the balustrade. Alone with Samya, who would stare at Rachida until she reduced her to a shadow.

On the way home from the cotton fields the men walked after one another in a file. They were tired and walked without talking. Suddenly, one of Rachida's cries fell among them like a stone, and some of the men heard it. Hussein, who always walked at the head of the line, stopped and said, "Listen, someone's calling for help."

"Nothing but a fight among the women," remarked Khaled, shrugging. His two wives were always yelling at each other.

Rachida's voice rose higher, like the whine of a dog baying at the moon.

"Something's going on," insisted Hussein.

The others, too, began to listen; they forgot their weariness. One of them suggested: "Let's go see what's happened."

"Yes, something's happening," repeated Hussein.

He began to run and the others followed him. Now they were all running. And when they saw other men far off in the fields, they called to them either to join them or to alert the people in the village.

As soon as the women heard cries for help, they too
dropped everything. Nefissa, who was too old to go with the
others but could read the future in the sand, repeated: "I
knew it! I knew that this day had the feel of misfortune!"

With their children the women abandoned the village to
Nefissa and the new-born babies. The men ran along the
path; they were coming from every direction: from their
small bouses, from the river banks, from the rice fields, from
the cemetery, from the garden, from the mosque.

Rachida saw them coming. Still leaning over the railing,
she lost awareness that she was screaming.

Everyone seemed to arrive at the same time, packed into
the narrow passage between the two houses. Their robes
brushed against the walls. A dull anger that they could not
yet explain thudded in their chests. Together, they seemed
to form a single body, and one could hear them cry out as if
with a single voice.

The room above seemed to lurch, tossed by this shout as
a rowboat is tossed by a wild sea.

*   *   *

The past burst into a foam of images that grew and threatened to swallow up everything.

The outcry of the crowd reverberated against the walls,
sounds sticking as tightly as the knots in a piece of string.
Ammal, who had left her flock of sheep, was squeezed in
among the others. She was small for her thirteen years. She
was wearing the yellow dress that Samya had made for her.
What was this uproar all about? Ammal was worried. What
had happened to Sit Samya? She battled her way through
the crowd; she wanted to be the first one to get to Sit Samya.

The old woman Om el Kher followed the crowd. Something was going on, something must have happened to Sit
Samya. Troubled, she wanted to go to the house to see but
not to ask questions of the others.

Farther off, resting against a tree, the blind man was worried, too. He wondered what had happened to Sit Samya.

Why was Sit Rachida shouting? It was impossible to make out what she was yelling over and over again.

The people were crowding into the house now while Rachida bent even further over the balcony to watch them push inside. She heard them coming up the stairs, shoving against one another as they climbed.

As soon as they reach the room Rachida will be able to collapse.

"If I had known! If I had known!" she will repeat over and over again. "I would have given up my walk. I would have given up petting the calf! I wouldn't have bothered checking the locks!"

The steps were narrow. The men and women were jostling and pushing one another.

Her hands pressed against her breast, Ammal came forward, murmuring, I only hope nothing has happened to Sit Samya! She tried to push through the people. She wanted to get to Sit Samya before the others, to save her. But to save her from what?

The clamor was becoming louder and more brutal. Maybe they would forget that the bannister was rickety. Maybe the stairs would collapse, and they would all fall. Maybe, too, there would be no stairway any longer. Rachida will stop screaming, and a person will finally be able to get some sleep.

But if they do reach the room, she will seize the past and hold it up between them and herself, creating of the past a watertight compartment. She will summon up the past and watch it unroll behind her as one follows a vanishing landscape through the window of a moving train. The past, she must recapture it, to hide herself in it!

But suddenly it seems so far away!

"Once I was a child, one day. . . . But I do not remember. Where is my childhood? And the face of my mother? Where is it? I can see nothing. I am in a very dark corridor, and I can't see anything. But much later. Yes, now I remember. I remember certain evenings. . . ."

* * *

Those Sunday evenings!

2 The car rolled through the city, its hood sleek and shiny, its windows closed. Inside were wood panels and dark leather. The house, the garden, the well-known faces were now far behind us. The car rolled past the shops, the street lamps, the sidewalks. It came to a sudden stop in the square which was dominated by the huge brown railway station; the station clock rang out the hours but they were drowned, lost, in the uproar of the streets.

Ali said that from this station trains departed for other countries, countries where, perhaps, there were no boarding schools. I had never been on a train; I had never been anywhere. Like so many other things, travel was reserved for grown-ups.

Tightly buttoned into his suit of shiny marine blue, Ali drove at top speed. I had to turn quickly and peer out of the rear window to catch a glimpse of the station, of the rushing passengers, of the porters, wearing long blue robes and loaded down with baggage. The streets were a confusion of bicycles, cars and donkey carts.

Ali drove so quickly! I hardly had time to look at the billboards, to try to catch the names of the streets, even to recognize the grain and spice shop in front of which, about a year earlier, we had had an accident. Having hit a bus, Ali had been forced to turn the car onto the sidewalk.

"Those people should be locked up! Bastards!" he had shouted. The grain and spice merchant had come to the front

of his shop, a starched apron tied around his waist. His lips
were trembling with emotion, but his plumpness and the
lopsided angle of his fez gave him an air of friendliness. He
had helped me out of the car.

"You have escaped! You have had a narrow escape!" he
exclaimed, guiding me into the shop by my elbow. He settled
me in a corner in a cane chair and brought me a glass of
anise and water in a pretty blue glass. I still remember every
detail. I managed to drink without making a face as the
merchant looked on, almost tenderly.

Out in the street Ali was examining the tires and the
engine. My brother Antoun, who always accompanied me
back to school on Sunday evenings, had leaped out of the car.
I could hear him discussing the accident with the gathering
crowd, his tone alternately friendly, alternately defensive.

Standing near me the merchant looked at me for a long
time. Perhaps he was imagining what might have happened,
for from time to time he clicked his tongue against his teeth,
clapped his palms together, and raised his eyes to heaven as
if he saw me there. "You have had a narrow escape," he kept
repeating.

When the car was ready to start again the shopkeeper
refused to accept any money. "No, no," he shook his head
firmly. Until the very last minute he went on expressing his
good wishes and giving us advice.

Ever since that day I have tried to catch a glimpse of his
door to give him a friendly wave. I have not forgotten his
kindness nor his tender face. But Ali was always in a hurry.
The doors of the boarding school opened at seven, and Ali
was anxious that I be on time. He drove quickly .....

Those Sunday evenings!

In the winters especially when darkness seemed to fall so
swiftly, and images of the city were reflected, distorted, onto
the gleaming hood of the limousine.

My brother Antoun accompanied me. He felt that it was
his duty to do so. At sixteen, he was reliable. Seated beside
me, he would dig into his pockets and bring out newspaper
clippings about stocks and bonds. Behind his gold-rimmed
glasses he read them with a serious air. Often, his mood
would become heavy, dignified, as if he were assuming the

years that would turn him into the man he was to become.
It was cold sitting beside my brother.

The car sped onward. I looked out at the houses. They fled
past at a dizzying pace with their crowded balconies, flowers
like patches of color hurled against the walls. The edges of
the sidewalks resembled hard gray lines sharply intersected
by alleys. With a sharp braking motion, Ali stopped the car
in front of a tall gate.

We had arrived at the school.

The murky flame of a solitary street lamp was reflected
against Ali's black scarred cheek. My brother shook off his
torpor and embraced me. Older than me by two years, he felt
obliged to give me some advice before giving me the bag
containing the sweets or nuts he always kept hidden until
the last minute. Nuts were forbidden, but Antoun never
remembered this. One had to be very clever to dispose of the
shells. His white teeth gleaming, Ali smiled as if to say:
"We'll be back to pick you up again next Sunday."

The gate was tall. I saw nothing but that. With the bag of
sweets in one hand and my overnight bag in the other, I
raised the latch with my elbow, pushing open the gate with
my shoulder. It gave way easily but instantly closed behind
me with a sharp metallic click. And now, where was my
brother? The motor car? The shiny cheek of Ali?

I tried to postpone looking at the heavy somber facade of
the school, which reminded me, somehow, of a widow's garb.
For a time I lingered in the garden, crunching the gravel
beneath my feet, imagining that they were pebbles of sand
at the beach. I wanted to turn back and run, to run, to open
the gate, to flee into the street. But where would I go?

I could hear the gate opening, then closing, the sound of
footsteps hurrying. How much longer could I remain outside? I took a few halting steps. Standing on tiptoe, I allowed
myself one last glimpse of the city.

Very tense, my shoulders tightly hunched up, I made myself go inside. The sister on duty at the door nodded as I
passed by. And then I was swallowed up in the corridor,
which seemed full of muffled whispers, and of silence.

Sometimes the idea came to me that I should simply let
myself fall to the ground and refuse to move. Perhaps every-

thing else would also stop moving then. But I was accustomed to following my own footsteps, and I walked on until I reached the coatroom.

* * *

All week my beret and my coat, which was too small, hung under a pink label which bore my name in neat proper handwriting.

My skirt was the regulation length. At home Zariffa had spent the day unstitching and restitching the hem. Because of her bad eyes she kept calling me to thread the needle for her. Then she made me kneel to see if the skirt touched the floor evenly. So my skirt fell correctly, and I could feel the stiff wool with each step. My black stockings were wrinkled around my ankles. In winter, I wore several undershirts beneath my blouse. My sleeves were too tight at the wrists, and my inkstained fingers seemed too long.

The doors of the cupboards squeaked when they were closed. A voice called the roll:

"Thirty-eight... Fifty-four ... One hundred and twenty-two...."

"Present. Present. Present." The voices seemed to be complaining.

"Fifty-six ... Sixty-eight.... One hundred and twenty .,-.."

"Present. Present. Present."

So practical for book-keeping, for marking the linen, for saving time. What did one do with the time that was saved?

The electric bulb gave off a weak light which blurred the framed image of a saint. The light was reflected on the varnished cupboards, playing over the grooves of wood, creating monstrous heads. Like flowers that open to the light, memories of home were beginning to blossom inside me.

"Fourteen ... Thirty-four...."

It was my turn: "Present."

I saw again the sunlight on the carpet; I smelled food and heard Zariffa's voice: "Go and get ready! Your father will soon be back!"

"Quickly! Quickly! Go get your veils, you'll be late," ordered the proctors, the supervisors, and nuns.

They bustled around, crossly, and the taps on their shoes went "click-clack" on the floor.

"Quickly! Quickly! Get your veils. Don't forget your veils. Don't forget your rosaries. Hurry up! Oh heavens! Hurry! Get in line for chapel. Silence, please."

In the classroom the half-open desks held notepads, textbooks, our black veils and our white cotton gloves. A few girls hid pieces of mirror among the wastepaper in their desks and tried to peek at their faces. I didn't want to look at myself. The veil hung down over my face, imprisoning me. The cotton gloves separated me from everything, even from the rosary whose rough wooden surface I liked to feel.

"Hurry! Hurry! Get in line! Silence! The same girls are always late!"

Josephine ran to her place, giggling. I was obedient. The veil, the black stockings, the walls. I couldn't shrug them away. I was suffocating. I would have liked to fight against all this, and yet I felt a strange fear. So I followed my own footsteps. I went forward with the others. I obeyed the commands. I remained within the ranks. I followed orders.

"Click-clack." The hem of my skirt beat against my legs. The ranks were tightening; there wasn't enough room for my shadow.

I moved along. "Click-clack." I heard nothing except this noise and the sounds of our moving feet on the large stones.

Once a year I went to the cemetery to place flowers on my mother's grave. My father, standing next to me, would bend toward me, place his hand on my shoulder and murmur: "It is a great loss for a girl!"

We advanced in a narrow file. The walls rose before us; they would never stop rising before us. And adults envied our youth.

*   *   *

The chapel always seemed to me so light, so high, so spacious.

"Click-clack." We had to bow down on one knee, make the sign of the cross, get up and enter the pews, organize ourselves, and then prayers rose from our lips at the same time. The prayers no longer meant anything to me; the words came to mind mechanically. I closed my lips tightly to keep the words from coming out. I hid my face behind my hands, and I dreamed of other words, of words that I knew existed but over which I would have stumbled if I had tried to pronounce them. I pressed my fingertips against my eyelids; I saw a world, another world, the world behind my eyelids: pink lights, revolving spheres, rose windows laced with light, petals of flowers and the plumage of birds.

After the prayers came the hymns. There was a different one for each day of the week. The melody penetrated my ears, distracting me. I looked at the statues of saints, at their dolls' faces, smooth, lacking the wrinkles, proof of our passage on earth. St. John's sheep had lost a foot. St. Theresa's flowers had faded. St. Peter's keys were broken. Bunches of artificial lilies stood rigidly in fluted vases.

The sanctuary was far away at the end of the earth, its golden doors double-locked.

Under a yellow stained glass window the old nun who looked after the toilets was kneeling, as squat as a dot. Before entering the chapel she had removed her black apron, and her gray dress stood out against the freshly polished benches. Her cowl was so tight that it wrinkled her face, making her look like a withered apple. She was slightly deaf and so to pray she pursed her lips with an air of concentration. I knew she had bright blue eyes, but because she spent so much time making clothes for poor children, she was beginning to go blind.

"I can't bear the idea of children being cold!" she had told me once. "It is unworthy of our Father." Then she had crossed herself three times to wipe out her blasphemy.

Her huge pockets were overflowing with her sewing materials; they made her black robes swell. Whenever she had a minute she pulled out her sewing and took a few stitches. I often watched her fat wrinkled fingers at work; her gold band ground into her furrowed skin.

Sometimes I longed to leave the other girls and their words, words made empty from over-use, and to walk alone down the central corridor carpeted in red. I would join the old sister, and maybe in her presence I would find the right words. Or maybe, in spite of my clumsiness, I might take some material from her pocket and try to sew. I would feel a little less useless, my heart a little warmer.

"Click-clack." The singing stopped short, cut off by the wooden sound.

"Click-clack." We had to leave the pews, bow with one knee, rise again, and file out in a neat row. Near the holy water fount I made the sign of the cross with the tip of my wet glove: "In the name of the Father .. .." I turned around. The old nun was still praying, shaking her head and mumbling. The girls laughed at her; she was probably repeating over and over: "Father, Father ... There are too many suffering children! What are you going to do?"

I would have liked her to remember me in her prayers, I whose undershirts protected me from the cold but not from myself. I came from a family with "social position." My hands were too fragile for me to fight for myself. I wanted to fling her an image of myself in the hope that she would catch it, place it with those of the other children, and send her voice rising on our behalf to this silent God.

When I left the chapel the little old nun was still wholly absorbed in her prayers. I left her and walked back into the corridor; it was eternally the same. Rosary wound around my wrist, I looked at the veil of Aida, who was walking in front of me. It hung to her waist; she seemed caught in a net. Once I had seen a struggling fish escape from a net, leaving scales stuck in the webbing. My brother had cursed the fish; he had leaned out over the water, spouting curses, while I stood next to him, my arms crossed and my hands pressed tightly under my armpits to keep myself from clapping.

*   *   *

Seven long days. Sunday evening. Monday, Tuesday, Wednesday, it was like entering a tunnel. Thursday was visiting day. My brother Antoun always came to see me; he was a man with a sense of duty. I would sit on a chair facing him; he would be seated in an armchair reserved for visitors. I was wearing my white gloves; this was required.

Antoun and I would look at each other; we had nothing to say. He was wearing a new striped suit and carefully pulled the pants up over his knees as he sat down. We looked at each other, we looked at the others. Josephine's pigtails were tied with satin bows. Aida was sucking candy. Her pockets were always full of sweets and naturally they got sticky. To clean them, she would turn them inside out and loosen the crusts of sugar with the tip of her pen. This work kept her entertained during the long dull hours of evening study. Leila looked exactly like her mother. Sitting close together, they had the same sad expression. They watched the clock with anguish. My brother also watched the clock; he always found a reason for leaving before visiting hours ended.

Friday. Saturday. Sunday underlined on the calendar with a red pencil.

All of this went around and around in my head while I sat at meals with the others at long tables, and later, too, in the dormitory as I lay behind the white curtains that enclosed our beds.

Leila was crying into her pillow.

"Sh!" someone said.

My own tears were not made of running water but of tiny grains that seemed stuck to my throat. Leila knew why she cried.

Why should I cry? For my mother, my thin-faced absent mother? In the photograph her eyes were lowered. Why should I cry? Because there were walls between people, between people and life? Because I felt imprisoned and couldn't understand why.

Sometimes sleep attacked me suddenly, and I would plunge into darkness. Sleep would seize me and hurl me into oblivion. And then—the brutal awakening when the horrible sound of the morning bell would fall upon my ears like pellets of ice!

At other times I waited for sleep to arrive. I was on guard. And when I felt it come close, I tried to savor it. I liked to feel it climbing up my legs to my chest and arms. I liked to feel it blurríng the curtains, the faces, the house itself, and even my grief, which had become senseless. My grief whirled away with everything else, dancing away on tiptoes. And then even Leila's sobs lost their meaning and I no longer sympathized with her need for tears.

My thoughts seemed to evaporate. They shrank to a single phrase, the sole bond which held me to life. I stayed on guard, for I wanted to remain conscious, to delay the moment when I would exist no longer.

In the morning sleep left me, a piece at a time, it seemed. This sleep came unstuck slowly, like adhesive tape from a sore. The shutters were opened. Footsteps glided past on the white marble floors. Sleep was growing accustomed to leaving me.

Josephine was the first to jump out of bed. I heard the sound of water splashing into her washbasin, then the joyous sigh she always made when she turned over her mattress. She emerged from sleep as if she had never entered it at all. She braided her hair, put away her things; then, secretly, she helped me make my bed.

She was so happy, Josephine! She accepted everything.

*   *   *

The windows of our classroom were so narrow we could barely see the trees. Winter turned into summer before we knew it was even winter. The seasons existed only in our textbooks!

Soad, who had wiry hair and freckles, was copying figures on the blackboard. Her mathematics notebooks filled us with admiration. She owned a box of colored pencils to help her embellish her work, which she underlined deftly with a ruler. Her calculations were as beautiful as drawings.

Raising an immaculate finger, the teacher said that I had an overactive imagination. My father said the same thing. He said that imagination led nowhere. My brothers laughed at my ignorance in mathematics and made fun of my compositions.

"Ha ha ha! 'Trees as bare as arms ...' "

"Soon we'll have to think about getting you married," said my father.

This concerned him much more than my studies. A daughter, what a problem! He was lucky to have only one! He was happy to know that I was at school where I was learning the essentials; this would make me easier to dispose of. But as for learning? He thought I already knew more than enough.

"As long as you can write a letter to your father telling him you've given birth to a son, that's quite enough," he would say.

All these births! All these baby boys people were wishing me even before I had time to wish for them myself! I was barely past the childhood they were determined to steal from me. Poor stifled childhood that was leaving me; it was defaced, dead, a space trapped between corridors that led nowhere, that opened onto nothing. Yet these thoughts gnawed at my heart: "Life is there! Life exists! It flows like a great river.... If you separate the yellow reeds, you will be able to see it."

"It is dangerous to go too close to the river banks where there are reeds," my father said once when we were taking a walk. "It is dangerous. A person can slip, fall into the water and drown!"

Soad was writing figures on the blackboard. In secret, Aida was arranging her hair; she was clever with her fingers. The teacher's bifocals didn't seem to help her see more clearly. To look like a devil, Josephine had made a mask out of violet paper; nobody was afraid of her.

Soon they would find a husband for me. I would have children. I must have them as soon as possible, I thought, as I slipped into the clear water of my bath.

A bath once a week. To conform to the rules, before entering the stall where the tub was located, I put on a long white shirt that covered me from my neck to my ankles. Only my arms were bare. We were instructed to scrub ourselves through the shirt so we would not have wicked thoughts. I had asked Soad, who always had an answer for everything, what this meant. She had launched into such a confused explanation that I had burst into giggles.

I scrubbed hard so the soap would penetrate my skin. The green water made the shirt billow out around my body.

In the courtyard there were trees growing in alternating rows. The ball whistled past my ear. I never got to it in time to catch it. Josephine just put out her hands and the ball would fall into them with a dry smack and nestle there.

Every thread of my dress seemed a weight on my body. I wanted to get away, to be alone, far from the others. I walked toward the lawn, searching for a glimpse of Amin, the gardener.

He always carried the hose on his back as if it were the empty skin of a serpent. He walked bent in two, his mauve cap embroidered in silk barely hid his bare skull. It was better not to get too close; Amin was protective of his flowers. He stooped down and talked to them in the tone most people reserve for children. He would urge them to grow faster, saying, "The season is nearly over!"

If he caught sight of a weed he would put down the hose, watching it from the corner of his eye as if he were afraid it might get away from him, and when he had to go very far, he would hang the hose up in the nearest greenhouse where it resembled a trapped animal. Then he would push his wheelbarrow in front of him, the earthenware pots clanking together as he moved.

"She's out!" somebody shouted.

A good catch was praised with cries of enthusiasm.

If you wanted to avoid this noise you had to go even farther away.

I liked to watch Amin. I would have liked to get even closer to the sound of the flower pots bumping around. I would like to have helped Amin rake the sand in the lane, push the wheelbarrow, water the paths and the pale grass, the pebbles, and the parched walls. I would have liked to feel the cool water on my hands.

Amin perspired so much that his robe stuck to his body. His feet were streaked with dirt. He was happy.

The bell rang. Josephine's cheeks were flushed with victory.

"I got five outs!" she cried.

Because she had violated the rule of silence, she was ordered to leave the ranks of walking girls. The smile faded from her lips, but it lived on inside of me. I did not turn around but I carried her punishment inside of my body, and it hurt.

*   *   *

On feast days Amin had to abandon his flowers. His hose then took on a menacing air, sputtering at his feet. If we got too close, he waved us back nervously. Rather than let us invade his greenhouses, he would walk back and forth dozens of times, carrying flower pots in his arms. He said that his plants would suffocate if too many of us came near them. He said that feast days were all right, but what about the poor flowers! It wasn't a feast day for them! He pestered us to take care of them for him, following us on his long bony legs all the way inside and as far as the central staircase.

Amin's flowers were not hardy enough to decorate the corridors we were walking through; a procession, we were dressed in white from head to foot, carrying candles that dropped hot wax on our gloves. Like us, Amin's flowers soon faded in this atmosphere of incense and candles.

The statues were adorned. The sisters looked like dark birds and when they moved their loose robes rustled like dry leaves. They were everywhere at the same time. One would have thought they had wings. Sacred music rose from one floor to the next. Josephine was wearing her special feast day face.

I dreamed that I was following my own funeral procession. I saw myself, so slim in my white dress, lying slender and lovely in death. I was wearing white gloves. (Zariffa had washed them hurriedly.) My hair was oiled so that it shone, even darker than usual. I was slender and white, lying in my coffin. An entire day was devoted to me; people were shedding tears for me. Jospehine was nibbling nervously at the gold medal that hung around her neck. Aida was rubbing the toes of her new boots together. Soad repeated my name over and over again. The nuns recited "Ave Maria" over and over again, monotonously. Amin came into the room with a pot of azaleas which he placed at the foot of my bed. My father's voice was sweet. He made the sign of the cross over my folded

hands. One after the other, my brothers kissed me on the
forehead. I could feel the tears in the corners of their lips.
This was my day! I was loved, and I forgot this feast day, with
its bland hymns, its odor of incense, the drooping flowers,
and the thought of Amin, who would pass a sleepless night
worrying about them.

Another feast day, that of the town, was celebrated twice
a year right under our windows. There were carts drawn by
small donkeys adorned with heavy necklaces of blue beads
to protect them from the evil eye. The carts were filled with
girls wearing brightly colored dresses, green, yellow, and
pink, colors that contrasted brilliantly with the black robes
of the older women. An ancient crone started singing, and
the others soon joined her, picking up the melody without
effort. Clapping their hands to keep the rhythm, they all
sang in unison. Sometimes their veils slipped off their shiny
hair, and they had to readjust them.

As the donkeys slowly pulled the carts forward, the wheels
creaked. A group of boys made a path between the carts
loaded with singing girls, trying to shove through the crowd
to the feast itself: fava beans, salted fish and green onions.

At this moment of exuberant happiness I longed to make
time stop! But the carts disappeared, swallowed up by the
next bend in the street and, one after another, they were
scattered over the grounds of the park where the girls got out
and sat on the grass, singing, laughing, talking as they
shared the feast.

From inside a voice was calling me. It was forbidden to
lean out the windows.

*   *   *

Sometimes one of us disappeared before the end of the
year. Her departure was surrounded with mystery. Later on,
we learned that she had gotten married. Then, one day she
returned with her husband to contribute a huge bouquet to
the chapel.

I myself dreamed of marriage now and then, of true marriage; my solitude would be consumed by a melting of souls.

I dreamed of a marriage which was made of love. The word itself had the fullness of a fruit, the sweetness and the juiciness. When I thought of it, I evoked summer evenings during which one bit into a succulent peach and was thirsty no longer.

I caught sight of Sarah as she was getting ready to leave us again: "I have been looking for you," she said.

We had sat together on the same benches, and yet I hardly recognized her. High heels, furs in which she seemed lost, brown suede gloves dangling from her fingers. The diamond she wore gave off a bright light. I no longer knew her. She was old and ugly, dressed-up this way.

Her husband also wore a ring, a diamond encircled with gold. Just looking at him, one could see the size of his bank account. He was short and fat, and his bald head already was shiny.

I felt like hitting Sarah, and yet at the same time, I wanted to hold her tightly and chase away this nightmare.

"You must come and visit me," said Sarah. "I'll show you my trousseau."

I was ashamed for her, for the way she had already given up. I was ashamed for her youth which demanded nothing of life. I hated her, but at the same time I wanted to clasp her tightly, to blow away the ashes and to breathe life back into her mouth.

Sarah was laughing. "You must all come," she said. And she talked about her huge house and her five servants. "I'll show you everything." She invited the entire class. "You must tell them, Samya. Some Sunday I'll send my chauffeur to come for you."

No, no, this will never happen to me. I'll resist; I'll hold on to my life. When I leave this place, I'll take charge of my life. That's certain. But suddenly I could hear my father's voice rising inside of me; it grew louder, amplified, resounding. His voice swelled until it swallowed everything else in the house:

"You'll marry him! ..." said the voice of my father. "You'll marry this man, or I will take a hand in it. And then we'll see!"

* * *

3 The arrival of Sunday brought the taste of hope to the tip of your tongue. Even though memories of past disappointments assailed you, after a week of waiting, one began to hope once again. On those mornings I brushed my dress and did my hair carefully. The passing hours had a meaning; they brought me nearer to leaving.

Ali was waiting in front of the gate. From the distance I could see his black profile, his fine features, his fez planted straight on his head. He was usually alone, but sometimes his son was with him, wearing long pants even though he was only ten. The son was darker than the father; the same scars striped his cheeks, three on each side. It was he who opened the door and got out in front of the gas station while Ali leaned on the hood and discussed politics or the weather. He held the same views as my father on everything; for more than fifteen years he had not left my father's service for longer than a day.

On Sundays around twelve we crossed the city again in the opposite direction.

The car rolled past streetlamps, past shops, past carts creaking along as if time did not exist. Trees, pavements and people were left behind. Nothing could stand firm against the motion of the car. Smoke rose from the railway station and mingled with the smoke of the factories, before dissolving above the rooftops.

Ali's back was immutable; not a muscle of his neck twitched. The car glided between obstacles, barely missed red lights, swerved sideways to avoid hitting a pedestrian. Suddenly Ali leaned out the window and yelled: "Son of a bitch! Wait till I catch you! I'll beat the life out of you!" Regaining control, he mumbled, "Sleepwalkers!"

The noises of the narrow streets mingled with the noises from the open balconies, growing thicker with each step of each passerby, with each new sound, taking on monstrous proportions before assaulting the public square. There this monstrous noise circled the equestrian statue, knocked on window panes, and swirled past a row of dozing carriage drivers. One could scream at the top of one's lungs; no one would hear. The noise was everywhere. Nobody paid any attention to it; it became a constant rumble, the tick-tock of a clock or the background music of a play.

The town flew by so quickly, it was nothing more than a succession of images drowned in this noise. The wish to capture these images one after another, to examine them, to understand them, these images of people, of forlorn facades and shop windows; this urge vanished with the car's flight. I was alone in the backseat, digging at the scaly worn leather with my fingernails.

The boulevard led to the house, which had a majestic air; two massive pillars supported the central balcony. At this hour my father and my five brothers were either taking a walk or chatting with friends on the terrace of one of the big cafés.

Hunched up on the bench, the porter was sleeping, barefooted; his Turkish slippers were lying on the ground. Nothing except the master's car could rouse him from his nap. As soon as it appeared in the distance, the very sound of the wheels seemed to pierce his eardrums. In less than a second he was standing up, his ivory turban straight, his slippers on, his hand ready to open the gate. He always kept his eyes fixed on a spot slightly higher than one's head, as if he were afraid his eyelids might drop of their own weight if he didn't hold them up by an effort. He slept all day long and sometimes in the most unique positions. His job consisted of opening doors and receiving insults from my father and brothers. Nothing affected him. He accepted their abuse with a great generosity of soul, eyes fixed on a spot a little above their

heads. Then, as soon as the car passed through the gates and
they were closed, he went back to squat on his bench.

Mardouk, the dog, howled when we arrived. He never recognized me. Ali had to use his most persuasive manner to
coax Mardouk to let me pass. "This is the daughter of the
house!" Ali would say. "Come, come, Mardouk . . .," he insisted gently. "This is Sit Samya, the daughter of the house."

The white marble staircase was covered with ants. They
were crawling over every step. Mardouk was so used to them
that he never hurt them.

Ali led the way, carrying my bag. The soles of his shoes
crackled as he crossed the gravel. Mardouk sniffed at the
hem of my dress. What was I doing here? Ali pushed open
the door, and I followed him into the big hall with the domed
ceiling. From this hall another marble staircase with
wrought iron railings led to the top floor. The bedrooms were
on this floor. Mine faced that other room, the one whose door
was draped with mourning crepe.

Ever since they had taken away my mother, her room had
remained intact, but it was kept double-locked, and the door
was framed by a large black border. For ten years now I had
felt the presence of my mother behind this door which I
longed to beat until it flew open. For ten years they had kept
her buried while I struggled to will her back to life.

"But the mourning period is over," said my father. "Soon
we'll repaint the door. We'll open up the room and fix it for
one of your brothers. The first one to get married."

The time was over, he said. She had to be dead, forgotten.
"Mother, Mother, my absent one, this black-bordered door is
my only image of you!"

My room was stuffy. When I opened the windows, clouds
of dust rose from the woodwork. I tore off my uniform and
threw it far away into the darkest corner of this prison, from
which I could not escape.

*　　*　　*

I could hear my father's voice as well as those of my brothers. All these voices echoed under the domed ceiling of the
foyer:

"Abdou! Abdou!"

My brothers were hungry. They wanted to go to the diningroom. My father restrained them, saying: "It is Sunday. We must wait for Samya."

I hurried. I took out my best dress from the closet, the one Zariffa had recently ironed.

"Samya! Samya!"

My name was resounding from the walls of my room. They were hungry. My dress was tight at the elbows, and I had trouble getting my arms into the sleeves. The seams ripped.

"Samya! Samya!"

They were threatening to sit down, to start eating without me. My father silenced them, and then he came to the foot of the big staircase and shouted up at me:

"Samya, my girl, your brothers are hungry. Hurry up! We are all waiting for you!"

I fought with the hooks. I didn't have time to change my heavy black stockings, and I couldn't help being aware of them as I walked down the stairs in my patent leather shoes. My hair had gotten messed up when I pulled on my dress; I hadn't the time to do it again.

"What a sight!" Karim mocked me, standing at the foot of the stairs. "I'm glad I'm only your brother."

The others laughed. "Well, you're finally here."

I ran but the staircase seemed endless. My father walked toward the diningroom, whispering with Guirguis, the eldest. They looked alike. Seen from behind, one could mistake them for each other.

Before sitting down I went up to each brother and each one kissed me on the cheek.

"You have grown again," my father said.

I sat on his left at the carved wooden table; my place faced the buffet with glass doors in which the silver was displayed. There were circles on the glass shelves where pieces had been taken out.

The Sunday meal consisted of a sauce of green herbs which we poured over rice, of onions, lamb, and chicken. My brothers and my father consumed huge portions. I also ate a lot, compelled by a feeling of rage.

Guirguis was over thirty. He had dark skin and cunning

eyes which enlivened his heavy drooping features. Although there were six years between them, Karim and Youssef were inseparable. They knew they were handsome, and they admired each other greatly. They discussed ties, women and cars. Sometimes they lowered their voices to spare me the details of their latest feats. Youssef was only twenty-two, but he already boasted of incalculable conquests and swore he would never marry until he was at least fifty.

"I," said Barsoum, "have decided to get married this year." And he asked my father if he knew of any young girl he could recommend.

My father liked to be consulted; he replied: "That's good, very good, my son. I'll think about it." He would find someone, he would go to visit my aunts, he'd consult the bishop.

Barsoum wanted a family; he would accept the wife his father chose but he wanted her to be young, very young.

"Certainly, my son, you must take a young wife, to train her."

Antoun was silent. He was the youngest but he looked so serious, with his growing stoutness and his gold-rimmed spectacles, that he was consulted in spite of his youth.

"What do you think, Antoun?"

"Do you have any suggestions?"

"One must marry young, don't you think so, Antoun?"

"It isn't necessary to marry before you're fifty, is it, Antoun?"

The conversation had taken off, and now "the family" was being discussed.

"Our cousin Souraya is over twenty and she's not yet married! Her brothers are so embarrassed they hardly dare to show their faces in society."

"Not yet married, in spite of her dowry!" affirmed my father.

"She's being difficult," Antoun commented.

"Difficult?" questioned my father. "You can see that no one's in charge of that household. My sister has no control over her children. If I took the situation in hand, you'd see a difference!"

"Souraya's strong-willed," Antoun reminded the others.

"Strong-willed!" exclaimed Karim. "She'll come to a bad end."

"A bad end," echoed Youssef.

Poor Souraya! Ticketed, labeled, and imprisoned by a rigid prophecy. "A bad end." But already the men were talking of other things. The price of rice was rising, business should be good. Souraya had to bear this shame because she wanted to choose for herself. The Fayoum cousins had earned three thousand pounds in a grain transaction. Cousin Hanna had made a brilliant marriage; his wife had brought him a fortune as a dowry.

"May God bless you equally, Barsoum," said Guirguis.

The faces around me no longer seemed human. I felt like getting up and stretching. Surely their masks would fall off, tumble to the ground and crumble into bits of cardboard. But I didn't move. I made myself as small as I could, deaf as well, so as not to aggravate the wound. I ate; I ate myself nearly to death, from revenge.

"Cousin Ghalil doesn't deserve his fortune. It should be taken away from him. He neglects his business to go abroad. He paints."

"Scribbles," pronounced Barsoum.

And to think I was made of the same clay! I was angry at myself.

Near the end of the meal their voices grew thick. Before bringing in the coffee, Abdou closed the shutters. He wore a white robe tied with a wide red sash which accentuated his slimness. My father loosened his tie.

"Samya, you'll go for a drive with Zariffa while we take a nap. Ali is waiting for you."

Upstairs, they were preparing the rooms for the afternoon naps, opening beds that had just been made up, drawing the curtains. Soon the house would be a tomb. There would be nothing but the sound of Mardouk's howls. Whenever a tram passed, he protected the master's slumber by howling.

Already my brothers were speaking less; their tongues were thick. They rose heavily without even looking at me. Only Antoun, who murmured in my ear: "I will be ready at seven to take you back to school."

My father was the last to move. He had trouble getting to his feet because of his weight. From the corner of his eye, Abdou watched him, alert, and at my father's signal, Abdou placed his hands under the man's armpits and helped him to his feet. My father hadn't energy enough even to bend over and kiss me. With Abdou's help he climbed the stairs slowly, already half asleep.

I heard the doors closing. I was alone under the arches. Sleep hovered around my head, weighing upon my shoulders, but then Zariffa appeared, her face leaden. Her voice barely reached me: "The car is here. We are waiting for you." She repeated the words, emphasizing each syllable. Without looking around, I could envision her bent head, the gray handkerchief tied around her hair, the way she pursed her lips when she spoke.

All the heaviness of the house fell upon me like a huge blanket, engulfing me, pressing me to the earth. With Abdou's help, my father was probably putting on his striped pajamas. For the third time Zariffa's voice called: "The car is here. Come on, you are wasting time!"

Later on, sitting next to Ali, she, too, would sleep, her head swaying from side to side.

Zariffa slipped the strap of my red bag over my shoulder. The bag was empty, except for a picture of my mother, the earliest one I had been able to find. "Come on," said Zariffa.

I followed her, descending the white steps slowly; my shoes were too tight. But suddenly fear of Mardouk made me quicken my steps. Once again, he would consider me an intruder.

I was an intruder. I followed Zariffa, old and gray, in her flat shoes, and I watched myself following her. What am I doing here?

I got into the car. The door closed behind me, and Zariffa seated herself in the front next to Ali.

*   *   *

The car moves along, and in front, between Ali's scarred cheeks and Zariffa's profile, the city dozes, torpid, languid, dozing beneath its blanket of dust. It breathes neither through its shuttered windows nor through its trees, whose leaves are limp. The car moves along, isolating me from the streets. But the streets knock at the windows.

Ali stops short in front of a half-open shop; the ice cream man never quite gives up the hope of catching a customer. Without much conviction he repeats: "Thirst keeps sleep away." It is Zariffa's mission on each of our Sunday outings to buy me an ice cream cone.

The pavements seem deserted, but as soon as we get out of the car a herd of beggars throws itself upon us. Zariffa insults them, waving her hands as if she were chasing away flies. They encircle us. I can see nothing but outstretched hands and shapeless rags, beggars encircling us, crying out plaintively.

Zariffa breaks through the circle, and I am left standing alone in the middle. I am ashamed of my expensive dress, of the car that is waiting for me. Zariffa's loud voice embarrasses me:

"Wait till I get back, " she shouts as she pays for the ice cream. "Just wait, you lazy beggars! You sons of dogs!"

I tremble; I wish she would be quiet. I would like to give them everything I possess, but my bag contains nothing but a photograph.

I would like to be one of them, to join them, to circle around Zariffa with these beggars, to roam around the city with them, through life itself, crying out, "Why? Why?"

"Lazy-bones! Thieves!" repeats Zariffa, who has apparently grown a heart of horsehair. Once again, she breaks into the circle, seizes my arm and drags me to the car. Without moving, Ali opens the door. I bury myself in the backseat, my head lowered.

"Lazy beggars! Thieves! Do you remember old Zannouba," asks Zariffa, turning around to face me. She gets in Ali's way, shaking her wizened head and wrinkling up her nose, Zariffa continues her tirade: "Always in the same place at the same time, old Zannouba! Everybody knew her. She was so skinny a person wondered how she managed to stand up. I felt sorry for her. How many piasters did I give her! The devil take her soul! When she died the neighbors contributed what they could to bury her. And do you know what they found under her rags?" She stops a minute and looks me straight in the eye; I know what she is going to say: "They found wads of money under Zannouba's mattress. Enough to

put up a mausoleum!" says Zariffa. "You should have seen
their faces, the neighbors! She was lying on wads of money,
like a beggar with crusty hardened feet turned outward, her
hand outstretched. She went to her grave like that, with her
hand outstretched!"

Zariffa goes on and on; there is not a trace of pity in her
voice. "Hand outstretched for eternity, in her tomb. That's
her punishment! A beggar for eternity! A good-for-nothing!
Enough to disgust you, the likes of her. Hey, Samya, do you
hear me?"

What do Zariffa's words matter? Beggars exist. True or
untrue? What does it matter? They are here. They go
through the motions of prayer over and over again. They
forget the rejections and the insults, and they go on endlessly.

"Do you hear me, Samya? Liars! Lazy-bones." She knew of
one who had hidden his gold in his wooden leg. Of another
who rented a skinny child by the week to attract people's
pity. "Sometimes they throw themselves under tramcars to
get their legs cut off!"

What do they matter, these tales? The beggars are here.
Their bones protrude like nails through the skin of their
chests. Instead of hands and feet, they have stumps. Eyes
drowned in misery. If they choose to do away with an arm
or a leg just to be pitied, is the shame theirs?

"Lazy-bones! Thieves!" goes on Zariffa.

And Ali, who is not talkative, adds: "Bastards, all of
them."

*   *   *

In the Avenue of the Flametrees red petals dropped onto
the hood, giving the car a festive air. They grew in clusters
the color of blood, blending with the sunlight. The flametrees bordered an island around which Ali drove slowly.
Slowly, very slowly. He wanted to fill out my Sunday. Ali
made the car trail along the banks of the river. We de-
scended, remounted, and crossed the steel bridges which

sometimes opened their monstrous teeth to let a felucca glide through, an image from another age. Far away beyond the grimacing banyan trees, lay the desert, waiting for the wind to break its chains of sand.

Zariffa's head dropped forward onto her chest. Her tortoise shell comb hung from her bun that was bristling with black hairpins. Ali stretched out the drive; we lingered near the garden with the mosaic columns, coasting alongside the opposite arm of the river. He let the time pass by.

I was eager to get back to the city which brought me the life and the movement that I lacked. But obscuring these scenes which I loved there was, nonetheless, always the reflection of myself which faced me in the window and from which I yearned to escape.

When we passed back through the city it had awakened.

The throbbing engines of cars, the cries of street vendors, the pleas of the beggars, the greasy laughter of the men sitting in the cafés, the squeaky voices of record-players—all this hubbub fell upon the city like the blows of a stick. The overcrowded tramcars could barely get through the traffic, in spite of the shrill whistles which the tram conductors blasted to warn the people who were loitering on the tracks. Three camels roped together were following a man who was abusing them. There was a donkey wearing a colored necklace. Shouting out headlines in three languages, newspaper boys were crossing the streets in all directions, shaking the freshly printed sheets under people's noses.

Ali was forced to slow down.

Passing by the shops was a woman with a huge cabbage balanced on her head as if it were a hat. Another was leaning against a wall, arms dangling. To me the people who were well-dressed looked as though they were wearing uniforms. I preferred the children who ran along, drawing patterns on the shop windows with their dirty fingers. In the side streets on crumbling pavements littered with vegetable skins boys were playing ball. Others were riding, four at a time, on a home-made scooter, clutching each other. The children seemed to become more numerous, to multiply like demons, mocking the vendors of fruits and vegetables who stood beside handcarts loaded with rotting produce.

Now and then a blind man miraculously made his way through the crowd without getting knocked down. He was trying to reach one of the rickety chairs in the shade of a crumbling wall.

*   *   *

The sky was growing pale, taking on new shades of light; it was time to go home.

We found the house empty. Mardouk didn't bark at me, but I didn't bother to pat him.

The silence of the house seemed thicker around my dead mother's room. Dead for ten years! Yet at each return I was startled by the black-bordered door.

Mother, my absent one! How many times I have carried you up these stairs, climbing laboriously to reach my room, your weight in my arms! Mother, my absent one, your death suffocated me. I climbed painfully, as if I were carrying you, my pale child, so heavy next to my heart. Like a stuffed doll, your body sagged between my arms, and you did nothing to make yourself lighter for me. Your cheek was cold against my neck. And your lips! Zariffa told me they were so white at the end that one could barely distinguish them from your face.

"Hurry! Hurry!" cried Zariffa's voice. "You are going to be late. You must be back at school before seven!"

I have only known you dead, my mother, my child! I remember that photo of you, the one in my red bag; you are twelve and you look frightened. I wish my arms were strong enough to protect you.

"Everything is ready. Your shoes are polished. Your dress is ironed. Don't dawdle." Zariffa's voice followed me. "Hurry up! Antoun will soon be here to take you back to school."

"Mother, you are so heavy in my arms!"

"Hurry up! Hurry up! You must be back by seven!"

Those Sunday evenings . . .

*   *   *

4 One morning the door was opened during the middle of class. It was the sister who served as concierge. Her starched white cowl, framing her face, shook slightly as she spoke. I must hurry, she said. I was wanted in the sitting room.

I looked for my white gloves; you never went to meet a visitor without your gloves. My schoolmates started whispering. Curiosity put some color into their pale cheeks.

"What can it be?" asked Josephine.

"Maybe someone at home is sick," suggested Soad.

"Or dead!" added Leila, who then hid her forehead behind her arm.

My brothers and my father were in good health. Only Zariffa, who was getting on in years. But if anything had happened to her, they would have waited until Sunday to tell me.

"Good luck!" shouted Josephine as I put my hand on the door. "Good luck," she repeated, defying the teacher who was demanding silence.

The corridor seemed endless. I didn't ask myself too many questions yet. One of the older girls was standing under the grandfather clock holding the copper gong; she was waiting for the hands to reach twelve when she would strike it with a mallet. This honor was granted to those who distinguished themselves by their piety. She caught sight of me and asked:

"Going to the sitting room today? What's the matter?"

I didn't know. I walked along the corridor without end, and I felt the girl's stare lying between my shoulder blades. I could have pointed at the exact spot where her eyes rested. I was beginning to worry.

In the sitting room I found my brother Antoun settled in an armchair whose red tassels hung around his legs. Leaning heavily on the armrests, he had such a dignified air that one would have thought he had just been decorated by his country for unusual patriotism. He didn't even take the trouble to kiss me.

"I'm taking you home," he said. "You're returning to the house with me. I've already told the sisters. You're being married."

Suddenly I realized how long I had been waiting, fearing these words, so remote and yet so near. To be confronted with them at last made them seem less monstrous. For the time being, brutal contact with reality kept me from thinking.

"I'll go and get my things," I told Antoun, who sat motionless.

The sister-in-charge had already given me the gracious smile that former students had a right to expect when they came back to visit on feast days. My brother's words had not yet had an impact on me. My classmates' questions were buzzing in my ears:

"So it's true?"

"You are getting married!"

"How old is he?"

"Do you love him?"

I answered without recognizing my own voice, a strange sound that came to me from the depths of an obscure and distant cave.

"I have known for a long time," I said, "But it was a secret. Yes, he is handsome. And I am happy! Sometimes he waited for hours just to see me pass by!"

I lied; I listened to my own voice. I was performing for myself as well as for my friends. I warmed to the game. "Yes, I'm going to be very happy!" I repeated.

As I spoke my words gave form to the abstract word "happy." I invented a face, loving arms that would keep my fears away, scattering them like pebbles.

"Yes, very happy!"

Could it be otherwise? My brothers, my father could not wish me to be unhappy. They loved me. It would be unworthy of me to imagine that my father had not chosen for the best. This man, I would love him, and he probably already loved me. No more nights passed behind starched curtains. No more wrenching awakenings. No more walls. I lied. My voice lulled us while we packed my things, my classmates and I. Our hands opened lids, lined the bottoms of suitcases with stacks of white linens. The scent of soap floated all around us.

"And your veil? Your white gloves? Don't forget them. Later, they'll come in handy for your own daughter."

These words shocked me into facing myself, suddenly, as if I had just awakened. I felt the soles of my feet on the ground. Straight and tense, I looked the sister in the eye, defying her. One day I would protect my daughter against her and these walls behind which one suffocated. My gaze bore through hers until she turned her eyes away.

"Your suitcases are ready," said Soad as she turned the key in the rusty lock.

Josephine clasped me around the waist.

"You won't forget me?"

Leila, Soad, Josephine, and Aida received permission to carry my luggage to the entrance hall. They walked with me. Josephine would not let go of my arm. My classmates were my only real memories. A lump rose in my throat at the thought that they had, in fact, already become memories.

"Poor child, she is upset," said the sister-in-charge to my brother, who was becoming impatient. "It is understandable. The girls become so attached to our dear house!"

*   *   *

When we were in the car Antoun quickly explained the situation at home. Business was bad. It was because of this that I had not been taken home the past three Sundays, not because my father was away, as I had been told. We had to act quickly now before people found out, sell what we could to pay off debts and arrange my marriage. If things got worse, it would become impossible to find a husband for me.

"But we have a prospect," added my brother, "the interview is tomorrow."

The house was in turmoil. The entrance hall and the main drawingroom were cluttered with furniture and my father came and went, waving his hands: "Here, to the right, is what is for sale," he was saying. "What I want to keep goes in the drawingroom."

His orders went in all directions, toward Ali, who was helping Abdou bring a chest of drawers downstairs; toward the cook and his assistant, who were dragging the old piano along. The porter, wide awake for a change, watched what was taking place as he leaned against a wall.

I began to understand what was happening more and more clearly. Bankruptcy had to be concealed. The rooms visitors never entered were being stripped bare in order to preserve the main drawingroom with its carpets and gilt furniture. They were getting rid of me too. I was in the way, I cost money. I must be married off as soon as possible. One must not lose face. There would still be guests and dinner parties; the house would remain "open." In this way we would be respected and could climb upward again, undertake new business ventures, keep up the dusty facade, a moth-eaten stage set, but imposing all the same.

To get to my father I had to thread a path through the heaped-up chairs, tables and various other objects. He seemed ridiculous to me, with his high-pitched voice and his fat finger pointing to one thing after another. "Ah," he said, spotting me, "Here you are!"

He went on giving orders: "No, no, Zariffa, you old fool! I've already told you, all of Samya's furnitue is being sold."

Zariffa was not sparing herself either; sometimes she even risked giving advice. Her attachment was boundless; she would never leave the family, even if they couldn't pay her. She asked only to be fed.

I tried to get close to my father to talk to him about what Antoun had told me.

"Talk to me, talk to me about what?" he snapped: "Can't you see I'm busy? Antoun has told you everything, hasn't he? The interview is tomorrow." Then he took a pencil from his pocket and handed it to me. "Instead of asking questions, make yourself useful. Get Zariffa to give you a sheet of paper and make a list of this furniture."

I still persisted. I had to speak to him. It was becoming more and more impossible to accept the fact that everything had been decided without even consulting me. I stressed my point. I wanted to touch my father, to make him feel my loneliness. If a part of him had really loved me, he would have been touched by the tone of my voice. I was close to him; his head was not much higher than mine, and put I my hand on his arm:

"Father!"

He turned away, reached for a crystal vase on a round table and addressed Zariffa: "This vase, Zariffa? It would be a pity to sell it. It looks so good on the marble sideboard."

"Father, Father!"

This time he got angry. I was a heartless girl, he said. My brothers and he had enough trouble. They spared me only because I was a girl, and here I was making things harder for everybody!

But I was determined to see him alone for a minute. I clutched at his arm. Zariffa kept telling me to go to my room before my father got really angry, but I pushed her away. My fingers tightened on his sleeve; he knew I would not give in.

"All right," he said, "Let's go into the study next door. But only for five minutes. I'll give you five minutes."

He opened the glass door and I followed him. The room had green curtains and the walls were covered with family portraits. My father took out his handkerchief and nervously dabbed at his mouth. He was angry at me for this insistence, which even I knew would be useless. Presently, my hope would fall back into my hollow palm.

We entered the study together, my father and I; then I closed the glass door behind us. A few minutes later we would come out again as if nothing had happened. The interview would still be tomorrow; I would marry the man they had chosen for me.

"Well, what do you want?" asked my father.

"Antoun has told me I am going to be married. It is so sudden, I didn't know what to answer."

"There is nothing to answer. Antoun told the truth. What more do you want?"

"That's not the point, Father."

"What is the point then?" He was at the door again with his hand on the knob.

"This man, I don't know him!"

"That's why there is to be an interview tomorrow." His voice was firm; he opened the door. "You are no beauty," he said. "Our affairs are going badly. If that gets around, you'll never find a husband. We'll have you on our hands forever." He added that he was not like his sister, Souraya's mother, that he would know how to use his authority to avoid having a leftover woman in the family. "Tomorrow your aunt will be here too. She is always on the lookout for a husband for Souraya; she hopes things will go wrong and she'll be able to give Souraya another chance. But things will not go wrong here. I have chosen you a wealthy man. You'll marry him. Otherwise, I swear to you, I'll see to it that you do!"

Everything had been said. We left the study. My father went back to his furniture. I went upstairs to my room. I spent the night sitting on the edge of my bed.

*   *   *

The next day the household returned to normal.

As she helped me with my bath, Zariffa told me everything she knew about my future husband. She scrubbed my back and poured scented oil into the water. The man came from one of the villages; he was the director of an important agricultural concern. He was forty-five, the perfect age for a husband. My father, too, got married at forty-five, and my mother was fifteen. "Like you," said Zariffa, her voice trembling with emotion. "Ah, Samya," she added, "how sad that she is no longer with us! Today she would have brought you the luck that is needed to please a fiancé."

Zariffa's gray forehead was bent over me and her gnarled fingers plunged into the water to catch the soap. I had trouble imagining life without her. Suddenly, I was afraid of life without Zariffa and the comfort she always brought me.

Under her brusque manner there was real tenderness, and I liked her hands, which had scrubbed and combed me since early childhood.

"Zariffa, I'm scared!"

"Scared? What are you afraid of? It is a good thing for a girl to find a husband. Look at me, what memories do I have? Only other people's memories. Don't be silly! You are going to be a lady and have children. Sons, if God blesses you as he did your poor mother."

Zariffa didn't understand my fears. And you, Mother, my distant, my helpless mother? Where were you? Did you wish for your marriage? Deep in your heart, did you truly long for it?

Zariffa dried me with a big towel and left me in my room. Soon she returned with a heap of dresses which she threw onto the bed: "They are all your size. Your father wants you to choose the one you like best."

One after another, I tried them on, but the dresses looked like they had been dug out of the ground, my face was so pale. Zariffa said suddenly: "This is the one that suits you best. I knew it would, because of the embroidery. I'll bring up your lunch and then you'll get dressed. The interview is at four. Your father says you must not be late."

The day went by slowly. One has to be patient, and then everything goes by. The worst lasted only a moment. The worst also passed on and was drowned eventually, along with everything else. One must have that kind of patience to wait for the end, either that or the ability to take action.

The day went by. The furniture was dusted, tea was prepared. Zariffa adjusted the sleeves of the dress around my thin wrists and when it struck five, she told me it was time. They had already been here for quite a while. I walked down the stairs, and through the door I could hear their voices mingling. Surely, they had discussed my dowry, my virtues, and the date of the wedding. I recognized my aunt's voice, my father's, and there was another, unfamiliar and dry. "That is Sit Rachida, your future sister-in-law," said Zariffa, who knew everything. Then she held me at the threshold for a moment while she made the sign of the cross on my forehead. In her other hand she held a small earthenware bowl con-

taining incense. "Wait," she said and she circled me five
times, uttering strange words. When she finished, she explained: "This is to bring you good fortune. Let's hope they
find you to their liking, the Bey and his sister, and conclude
the arrangement."

Then she took me by the shoulder and gave me a slight
push toward the drawingroom. The door was opened by an
invisible hand.

*   *   *

They were sitting in a circle. Facing me, a woman with a
low forehead tightly bound with a black scarf knotted at the
nape of the neck. Two staring eyes, spider's eyes that seemed
to undress me. I felt like raising my hands to protect myself.

"Come here, come closer," said the woman with the spider's eyes. I could no longer escape them, or her tight mouth.
I stepped forward and my father's voice introduced me, saying:

"Here is my daughter, Samya. Samya, this is my dear
friend, Sit Rachida."

In an effort to smile the woman's face collapsed into a
thousand creases like a sail falling in on itself. I said nothing,
and my father explained: "Young girls are so shy!"

My aunt's voice rose: "A sign of good manners. Take my
daughter Souraya, for instance. You wouldn't know the color
of her eyes, they are always lowered. Poor angel! A model,
my Souraya, a true model of a girl!"

I held out my hand to Sit Rachida, who pulled me toward
her, making me bend down so she could kiss my forehead.
Then she said: "Boutros, look how charming she is!"

I didn't want to look at this man. He was behind me. So
his name was Boutros! Maybe he was different from the
others. A ray of hope crossed my heart like a murmuring
breeze.

I kissed my aunt and asked about Souraya, keeping my
voice low. She answered loudly, for everyone to hear: "She
is so busy with her needlework now! She does wonders! My
Souraya, what a perfect housewife she is! You don't find girls

like her nowadays. When she plays the piano, you think you are in paradise. Isn't it so, my brother?"

She beamed at Sit Rachida, but my father turned away without answering. My aunt's kiss was like ice on my cheek. In turn, I kissed each of my brothers. They were bored and blamed me for this wasted afternoon, but they tried to give the impression that they were going to miss me and that my future husband was a fortunate man. Guirguis, who was sitting on my right, was talking to the man. Their voices were blurred. With my feet still glued to the floor I moved around the circle. I greeted Guirguis, and then I could no longer put off meeting the man. His legs were next to my brother's legs. His feet were small, and the smell of shoe polish floated around his yellow leather pumps. I held out a hand which did not seem to belong to me, a doll's hand, empty. The palm into which I let it rest was fat and moist. I felt that the man was making an effort to stand up.

"Be seated. Please, remain seated, my Bey," protested my father.

The man did not have to be told twice. I saw his large stomach, spanned by the chain that passed from one waist-coat pocket to the other. His left hand was playing with amber beads. I could guess at the face. Nonetheless, the length of his nose surprised me. Buried in the mass of his cheeks, his eyes were small but as quick as rat's eyes under creased brown eyelids.

All around me voices were whispering. "Samya, my dear, please pass the cakes."

I picked up the dish and went from one to another, feeling the spider's eyes and the rat's eyes following me. Then I sat down in the empty chair between my aunt and Sit Rachida. Leaning on his elbow, my father was confiding in her: "Her poor mother died so young! I have had to look after every-thing myself. But I have taken care of all her needs."

Sit Rachida nodded approvingly.

My father went on: "As for her health, there is nothing to say. She is built like a tree. She'll carry only boys! A strong girl! You've only to look at her to see. Samya, my little Samya, would you open the window? Sit Rachida is too warm."

I walked to the window at the other end of the drawing-room, knowing what they wanted, and their eyes followed me. In an attempt to focus her brother's attention, Rachida said: "You see, Boutros, they have a view of the boulevard."

They were all watching me. I was neither lame nor deformed. My aunt leaned nearer to Sit Rachida and whispered in a condescending tone: "Yes, she's quite attractive."

My brothers were losing patience. They had talked of the harvest, the cotton worm, the rise in prices; they were squirming in their seats. Addressing me, Boutros asked if I had pleasant memories of boarding school.

I answered affirmatively. I was trapped into lying. Lies kept their houses glued together, as well as their lives and their hearts, and more lies entangled my life with theirs.

Sit Rachida and Boutros had seen me and had heard my voice. They could leave now. "Boutros," said Sit Rachida. "I'm afraid it's time to go now."

They all stood up. Sit Rachida pressed my father's hand insistently as if to assure him of her support. The goodbyes were cordial. My aunt, realizing that it was settled, looked glum and left without kissing me. Souraya would have to put up with her whining all night. Which of us two was the more to be pitied?

The man called Boutros bowed low to me. For a minute I thought his fez would tumble off his head and roll away.

Together, we accompanied the guests to the garden gate. Ali was waiting at the open door of the car. From behind the shutters Zariffa was surely watching and rubbing her hands in glee. To marry off a daughter was a wonderful event!

"It is Sit Rachida," said Zariffa when the phone rang an hour later to confirm that everything was settled. She held the receiver to my father and threw herself upon me, showering me with kisses.

That night I slept.

I was sheltered behind another me, one who had come without my calling for her. She was another person and yet myself. When things became too heavy to bear and inside me everything seemed to disintegrate, she came to help me. My own vitality seemed to ebb away from my arms, my legs and my voice.

The next morning when Zariffa opened the door to say, "Your fiancé and his sister are coming to take you for a drive," I still felt protected. Voices came to me from afar, hitting the other me like balls thudding against a padded wall. Noises lost their sharpness before they reached me. I was absent and yet I observed things.

"Part your hair a little lower," Zariffa suggested. "Don't fasten your belt so tightly." And, later, "Smile when you speak. A wife with a sour face makes a husband grind his teeth."

"But don't talk too much," she went on. "Girls who talk too much are trying to conceal the black cat hidden in their hearts."

I changed the part in my hair again. I loosened my belt. I nodded. I was nothing but these gestures. How relaxed I felt! If I could always feel like this!

In the afternoon Zariffa came to get me. They had hired a horse and carriage and were waiting at the front gate.

Sitting between Sit Rachida and her brother, I was not ill at ease. Their voices rose and fell, passing before me like wisps of grass. The horse's hooves tapped sharply on the asphalt. Their voices were low. They started off again, directing questions at me, smothering me with questions. When would I be sixteen? What childhood illnesses had I had? Typhoid? Yes? And measles? It sometimes leaves after-effects. And my brothers, what serious young men! It is a lucky father who knows his fortune will be left in such good hands. As a matter of fact, how many stores did my father own? And servants, how many do we have?

I answered as if this accounting did not concern me at all. I was lulled by the slow pace of the carriage. The driver's back was a black screen between the sun and us, and I felt absent and invulnerable.

The whip cracked. The horse trotted past donkeys, avoiding cars, and sometimes let a bicycle get ahead of us. Bound by leather straps and wearing little cotton bags to protect his ears from flies, the horse trotted through the city streets, along the banks of the river and through the Avenue of the Flametrees. His hooves struck the pavement with heavy monotonous thuds.

"And your dear father," asked Sit Rachida, "is he happy about the way business is going?"

"Very happy."

At the crack of the whip the horse trotted faster.

"How he must spoil you! What surprises does he have in store to celebrate your wedding? Did your mother leave you any jewels?"

"I don't know."

"Move along, move along!" cried the driver, letting the whip play over the horse's ribs. He held the reins firmly, and I felt that this horse no longer knew how to neigh.

"And your brothers," went on Sit Rachida, "what are they going to give you for a wedding gift?"

"I don't know."

"It is so embarrassing for young men! Ask them for jewels. They never lose their value. They remain eternally valuable."

"Yes, I will ask for jewelry."

The driver fidgeted with the reins even though the horse obeyed even the slightest motion of his wrist. Left, right, forward, slowly, more slowly still. One could make him do anything, no matter what.

"Yes, Sit Rachida, I'll ask for jewelry." I'd ask for jewelry, I'd ask for whatever they wanted. I didn't feel anything at all, neither pain nor sadness. I'd do anything. The horse's hooves were making a deafening noise.

"Faster, you son of a bitch!" yelled the driver.

"You should have a diamond ring," said Sit Rachida.

Boutros was smiling at me. I smiled back. I looked furtively at the box of candy in the shiny paper tied with pink ribbon that Boutros held on his knees. I knew it was for me. The driver had stopped under a grove of trees. Climbing down from his seat, he offered the horse lumps of sugar from his palm, calling him "my brother."

"Eat, eat, my brother," he said.

"About your wedding dress, I'll be there when you try it on," said Sit Rachida. "Like an older sister. Yes, that's it. From now on I am your sister. Call me 'Rachida,' "

*   *   *

On the way back I gave myself over to the swaying of the carriage. The sun burned my knees through my dress. The roads were empty, so the horse maintained a regular pace, but as soon as we reached the city we heard an indistinct murmur that seemed to come from the distance. The horse trotted on. Suddenly, sharp cries intermingled with the murmur. Rachida asked the driver what was happening, but he only shrugged.

Suddenly we came to a sharp bend in the road and the noise grew much louder. Men were running along the sidewalks. We were caught up in a tangled mass of cars, carts and people. The driver made the horse stop. The carriage was roughly shaken. Rachida became frightened; she shrieked and clutched my arm, exclaiming: "Holy Virgin! Mother of God!"

People were pushing one another so they could see better. Curious frightened faces were thrust out of windows. Not knowing what attitude to take, Boutros starting abusing the driver who, in turn, vented his rage on the horse. But this time the horse stiffened. Throwing off his torpor, he rose on his hind legs and swung his tail savagely, struggling to free himself from the harness. I, too, had stiffened, grasping the driver's seat. I could see the veins sticking out like ropes on the horse's neck. My muscles were tense. The horse neighed as he reared. He seemed to be facing danger. The driver had lost control of the animal; he jumped down to seize the bit.

The crowd was growing even more agitated. People were coming from all directions to join the curious mob.

"What's happening?"

"An accident?"

"A crime?"

I could hear questions crossing one another in the confusion. The boldest edged their way forward to get a better look. At the end of the street gray smoke was rising. Where was it coming from?

I got down from the carriage, followed by Rachida and Boutros who were holding onto each other. Quickly, I left them and became part of the crowd. The veil that usually sheltered me from the world was gone. A cry of distress seemed to come from the distance, and the idea that I might be able to do something made me push forward. Nothing could stop me.

I advanced through the mass with a thousand heads. I had to get to the center of the crowd. Something was going on. Surely something was going on.

Near me I heard people talking about a man. A few minutes earlier he had been seen running, and his clothes smelled of gasoline. It was to this man that I was running. I had no time to ask questions. My apathy had left me; I was panting.

"A madman!" someone cried.

"A revolutionary!" cried another.

Always I kept on running. Voices came from all sides. I heard them as I frantically pushed and shoved my way through, terrified that I would get there too late. Somebody said the man had just set fire to his clothes and that he was now burning like a torch. He was in the middle of the street. He had set fire to his gasoline-soaked robes. He wanted to put an end to his life.

"Madman! There are too few hospitals," a woman shouted.

Another said that suicide by fire was becoming very common but that a gun was much simpler.

"A gun is too expensive," a voice cut in.

"He'll go to hell. It's hell for him," shouted somebody; it could have been Rachida.

I kept on running. It was hot. I made my way through the motionless cars and bicycles and all those people who were pressed together, asking questions and wondering. The man who was burning had seven small children and his wife had just died. Someone said he was a coward. Then another voice cried out:

"He is burning like a torch!" The words were swallowed by the noise of the crowd.

I listened. I kept running, always, trying to imagine the unknown face of this man who was dying.

"He has no job!"

"He is lazy!"

"Lazy good-for-nothing!"

The voices rose together, cutting against each other; everyone had something to say. They complained that the city was swarming with beggars. Words originating in the distance were passed from mouth to mouth. Those who were closest to the man were shouting: "He's burning like a torch. He's writhing. He's screaming: 'Let everyone watch! Let everyone watch me die!' "

I had lost Rachida and her brother; I was moving through the crowd with difficulty. Next to me somebody was crying. All of a sudden I was pushed back roughly: "Get back! Get back!" people were shouting. A woman fainted. People were worried about the fire spreading. The crowd kept me from going forward, and yet I knew I should be over there near the man who was dying. I wanted to leave the weeping women behind me. What good are tears if one dies alone?

The man must not die alone. I walked toward him in a kind of rage. I could hear his cry: "Let everyone watch me die!" This death, which was intended to be striking, was paralyzing the city. But long before the day was over, it would fade from people's hearts. Maybe he knew this already. I wanted to get close and drive away this thought, to be the last understanding face he would look upon. To die might then be easier. Would nobody try to understand what dying really meant? If they understood they would end this farce, and there would no longer be this immense net of indifference around this world in which the best seemed doomed.

Before I could get any closer, someone cried out: "It's over." And yet I saw him, this man, as if I had been at his side. I saw him fall like a heap of charred clothes dropping off a line.

People were carrying away buckets of water. Women were wailing. I could hear a siren. The street had to be cleared. The police were arriving; soon we would be on our way again.

A hand gripped my shoulder; I heard Rachida's dry voice: "We've been looking everywhere for you! What an end to our drive! So he wished to burn! Well, he'll burn for eternity now!" I wanted to bite the bony hand that encircled my arm. Boutros took hold of my other elbow and they pulled me along with them to the carriage.

Again I was caught up in what is called "life." I walked along between Boutros and Rachida, framed by Rachida and

Boutros. The crowd had broken up; the traffic had begun to move again. We saw the driver; he was waving at us with a bandaged hand. "This way, this way," he shouted. When we got nearer he started to complain that the horse had bitten him. He didn't understand what sudden rage had come over the animal. Such a docile horse!

Once again the three of us were sitting in the backseat. The carriage turned into an alley to take a shortcut home.

"The Virgin Mary was with us!" exclaimed Rachida. "We could have tipped over." And Boutros crossed himself in approval of her words.

I said nothing; head lowered, searching for the memory of the dead man, I found myself as well. We were both dead, we two suicides, that man and I. Images of his brutal death and my own slow one spun around and around in my chest. I bowed my head in mourning.

We had reached the house. I got out of the carriage, said goodbye to Boutros and goodbye to Rachida, but all of this was no longer important. Boutros gave me the box of candy and I said "Thank you." I held the box against my body. I heard the horse's hooves; the carriage was gone.

At last my tears began to flow. They soaked the shiny paper which covered the gold box decorated with brilliant gold coins. I was still in the garden. I walked up the steps. Zariffa greeted me at the door, exclaiming:

"The joyous tears of a fiancée are as sweet as honey!"

* * *

Part Two

It was our wedding day. We had come by train. Abou Sliman, Boutros's servant, was waiting at the station to drive us to the farm. I was still wearing my white satin dress.

5 Through a shortcut we soon reached the open country. It spread out in a flat pattern that was broken now and then by the sail of a felucca. The trees leaning over the water were caressed by the breeze. Boutros was asking the driver questions.

The road stretched out before us. It passed over a bridge and was swallowed up by the fields like a dusty ribbon lost among the green spaces. Farther on, it branched off between rows of young banana trees and became a gravel lane that made the carriage shake. Finally, it ended between two houses that stood facing each other across a narrow passageway. Boutros pointed to the one on the left.

"That's our house," he said. "Here is the key. Go on up to the second floor. I'll join you later when I've seen the employees in the office. Just nod as you pass them."

The five clerks were waiting for us on the doorsteps. They were whispering and rubbing their hands together to make a good appearance. With the veil over my arm and a crown of orange blossoms around my wrist, I had to take tiny steps because of my tight skirt. I greeted each one in turn, noticing that one had a huge wart at the corner of his eye. They returned my greeting before offering Boutros their congratulations.

In church that morning the priest had given me to this
man and he had blessed us as if we had been created for each
other. My "yes" had been enough for him to hand me over
to this man with words that chained me for eternity. How
little he had cared about me or about his own words, so heavy
to bear! He had chained us and our children and grandchildren up to the fourth generation. Then he had solemnly
departed.

I belonged to this man who had been imposed upon me. At
the threshold, his harsh voice assaulted me. I heard him
questioning the clerks, asking if anything had happened in
his absence.

I went up the stairs toward this man's door, toward his
room, toward his bed; I climbed laboriously. The silk of my
skirts clung to my legs, making it difficult for me to walk,
and I felt trapped between the voice at the foot of the stairs
and the room above. The staircase was lighted only by a dirty
skylight. Just this skylight but then, suddenly, a child's
laughter.

It was as if someone had shaken tiny bells. I looked about
and found her huddled in a corner of the landing. She had
dark black eyes and wore a red handkerchief tied low across
her forehead. Her nose, cheeks, mouth and chin were laughing. She was laughing at me, at being there and at being
discovered. It was so good to hear laughter that I joined
in.

But the child was already on her feet. She pushed me aside
and ran down the stairs without looking back. She took our
laughter away with her, down the stairs through the open
door and she disappeared.

Later, the moon shone brightly, outlining everything in its
pallor. This moonlight made it easier for me to remove myself from this man who was lying beside me.

At times I clenched my teeth, but soon the night drew me
to it once again with its pale light which lifted the weight
of the day from each piece of furniture. The high window
which opened onto the balcony framed three stars. They
seemed so close that had I stretched out my arm, they would
have fallen into my palm. Their warmth would have protected me from the panic which seized me each time I re-

turned to this sweating sighing man, whose mannerisms deepened my hatred and to whom I watched myself submit with such cowardice that I was disgusted.

I tried to imagine the countryside spread out around us, this countryside which I was never again to leave. I tried to love it through embracing the night that entered through the window. In spite of the darkness, the sky was strangely transparent, as if it were made of layers of veils that might blow away if the breeze rose. The bedsprings creaked. I wanted to think only of the night, bathed in star light and moonlight and of the sweetness of this night which flowed into my room. The bed creaked, the body twisted and turned, making noisy sighs that broke the silence. Facing him once more, I clenched my teeth so hard I thought my face would crack into pieces.

But I was rescued by a song, a song as fluid as a slender silken thread. I recognized the voice of the little girl who had been hiding on the landing, laughing. "Night, oh my night," she sang. The same girl I had found curled up on the landing. I imagined her now, leaning against the house, head thrown back as her song rose and fell against the walls. The night was so beautiful she had left her bed to admire it. "Night, oh my night!" she sang. The notes of her song fell onto the sun-bleached stones and soared into my room like drops of dew, making the room seem larger, carrying it off into the night. My room was floating outside in the serene country-side far from the bed in which I found myself. For a moment I forgot its horrible squeaking.

"Bitch! Bitch! I'll teach her to keep people from sleeping!" Propped on one elbow Boutros was shouting feverishly. He threw off the sheets and was about to jump up: "I'll teach her!" he kept repeating. His voice crushed her song and I could hear only an occasional reckless note. Before he could move I was at the foot of the bed.

"Don't bother. I'll go. We won't hear anything now." I hurried to the window and closed the shutters. I drew the curtains. The child's song still reached me, but now only as a murmur. Yet I knew it was still alive and I felt that I had protected it from a threat. Suddenly, Boutros's oily laugh burst out:

"So, she disturbed you too? Come, don't worry. The night is still young!"

The real night had been shut out with the stars and the child's song. I hadn't moved from the window. Boutros was calling:

"Come on, come on! Hurry up! What are you waiting for?"

What was I waiting for? For the impossible. Perhaps for the end of the world. My bare feet stuck to the floor. I tried to gain time, repeating: "It's so dark. I can't see." But Boutros was getting impatient:

"Hurry up!"

When I reached the foot of the bed I hesitated again. He caught me roughly by the hips and pulled me down next to him. The bed squeaked worse than ever before. I bit my lip so hard blood ran into the corners of my mouth.

The next morning I went onto the balcony to look at the countryside. It spread out behind the house opposite, the absent landlord's house. It was very flat land, and it emerged slowly from the dawn, languorously. Along the paths men were walking, hoes over their shoulders, walking in a single file that looked like a gray ribbon. Topped by round leafy balls of foliage, the trees looked like sticks which would be uprooted by the first wind. The young sun played among the green fields, ruffling the stagnant water of the canal and falling upon certain stones. Not even one small valley broke the smooth landscape which ran along the insurmountable wall of the low-lying sky.

Like this countyside my life was spread before me. This inevitable life. What could I do to change it? I would have to stop complaining. Pregnancies would come, one after another, to prevent me from worrying about myself. I was dreaming of this as a refuge and yet, at the same time, I shuddered to think of a child born of these nights when I desired only death.

"One has to take things as they come," Josephine used to say. I only wished I could do it. I unpacked, opening the armoire to hang my clothes in it. My books were dusty from having been stored away in a closet ever since my mother's death. I carefully dusted them before putting them on the shelves. I arranged my belongings. Then I tidied the room and looked for a place to store the empty trunks. Somebody knocked on the door.

Before I had time to open it, two women in black robes and veils were standing in the middle of the room:

"I am Om el Kher," said the older. "This is my daughter, Zeinab. We'll bring you eggs and vegetables every day, just as we did for your sister-in-law, Sit Rachida, when she lived here with the Bey."

I thanked them and took the basket they held out to me, but they remained fixed in their places, staring. I felt they would like to take me in their hands as if I were a toy and turn me over and over, to finger the material of my dress, and to touch my hair. Awkwardly, I put down the basket next to a table on which there was a box of candy. I handed it to them, saying:

"Here, these are for you. Have some sugared almonds."

They stepped backward, shaking their heads, simpering: "No, no, they're yours," they said in a single voice. I insisted, and they came forward again and touched the box, but they repeated: "No, no they're yours. They are for you and the Bey! May Allah bless you and grant you a long life!"

As they were still hesitant, I poured some of the almonds into their hands. The women thanked me profusely, laughing in confusion. They slipped the sweets into pockets concealed in their robes, smiling at the rattling sound of the candies.

Om el Kher whispered something into her daughter's ear and starting pulling at her bosom to remove a safety pin with a blue stone in it. "Take it," she said, offering it to me. "It is for you. It will guard you against the evil eye. You and the Bey."

It was my turn to feel confused.

"For forty years I have worn it," she explained. "Ever since the day of my marriage. Now I am too old to be envied. But you ..."

The rusty pin had left two holes in her robe; she tried to fill them in by rubbing her nail over them. She then helped me pin the stone to my blouse, adding with a sigh of relief:

"Yes, wear it where it will be seen, to put the evil eye to shame!"

To show my gratitude I threw myself into her arms. Om el Kher pressed me against her; her robes smelled of earth and henna. I felt very calm and, at the thought of these moments that are like bridges between people, I told myself that everything would work out all right.

"Well," said Om el Kher, "so you are happy now!"

She felt familiar with me now and gave me friendly taps on the shoulder. Then, her hands on her hips, she stood waiting for me to confide in her. Zeinab nodded to approve each of her mother's words or gestures. She was soon attracted by the pink satin bedspread and she went over to it, slowly, unable to keep her eyes off it.

"So you are a bride now, " continued Om el Kher.

It was up to me to talk, and so I invented things for her, as I had done for my schoolmates, describing a happiness I had never known. Cleaning her hands on her robe to rub off the dust, Zeinab then placed them on the shiny satin; one could almost see the shivers running up and down her back as she stroked it.

"I was twelve when he saw me for the first time. I was still in school. I was too young for him to ask my father for my hand."

"In school?" echoed Om el Kher. "So you can read and write like the clerks in the office?"

"Yes."

"I don't mean to offend you, but what good will that be to you now?"

I asked myself the same question but not knowing what to answer, I went on: "He wrote to me every week. On feast days he sent me flowers!" I talked on and on. I forgot Boutros. Zeinab lost interest in the bedspread and came nearer to listen as I described my wedding and my father's despair at the thought of my leaving. I told them about the moving speeches with which my five brothers had entrusted me to my husband. Om el Kher and Zeinab devoured me with their eyes. My lies transformed Boutros's puffy face, his harsh gaze, his heavy body, rocking slightly on the ridiculously small feet he always kept a little apart. The image of another man, one I didn't even know, was born in me and filled the room until the moment when the doorknob turned and a voice shouted:

"Still here, you women! Go! Out! You are tiring Sit Samya. Come on, out of here! Go back to your houses!"

They looked like guilty little girls as they gathered up their robes and disappeared without even saying goodbye to me.

I watched Boutros. Words dried on my lips. He was staring at the blue stone pinned to my blouse.

*　*　*

I never forgot that first day. A little later, Abou Sliman, Boutros's servant, arrived. He came into the living-room and bowed respectfully before me, then he went into the adjacent room.

"Besides being our driver, Abou Sliman is our cook," explained Boutros. "He is used to my tastes. You don't have to do anything. Just let him do as he wishes. Today," he went on, "I came home unusually early. One doesn't get married every day!"

He settled back in the green armchair, drew his amber beads from his pocket and let them slip slowly through his fingers. His fez was pushed onto the back of his head, uncovering his glistening forehead on which there were always beads of sweat. Boutros weighed heavily in the chair, his heels barely touching the floor, his toes pointing upward. His left hand was playing with the polished amber beads, fingering them listlessly.

"I was unable to find that girl's name."

"What girl's name?"

"The girl who sang under our windows last night. But someone will tell me. I'll go around the village this afternoon, and I'll find out her name."

I asked him not to think about it any more. It was not important. We had only to close the windows.

"Close the windows!" he repeated, adding that I must be losing my mind; he had no intention of giving in to whims. "This afternoon I'll go the village," he went on, "I'll find her father and get him to punish her. I assure you, she won't try that again!"

I insisted that he forget it but Boutros said his mind was made up. "Anyway, it's my business, don't interfere."

Abou Sliman served the rice dish. He had replaced his jacket with a long blue apron tied over his robe. He had laughing gray eyes that didn't seem to belong to his knobby face. He returned with huge portions of food which Boutros devoured, making noises with his tongue. His lips and chin were greasy.

Abou Sliman seemed to be everywhere at the same time. Boutros called him to refill the salt shaker, then to pour water from the jug which stood on the table, and again to pick up the napkin which had slipped to the floor.

Time passed.

It was the hour for the siesta; Abou Sliman walked about on tiptoe, drawing the curtains, closing the shutters.

At this moment thousands of similar preparations for sleep were being made, for sleep itself was descending over the entire countryside. Sleep was conquering villages and towns. Those who possessed shutters were closing them; the others, far more numerous, had to be satisfied with closing their eyes. Sleep seized people by their necks, grasped their shoulders, forcing them to bend forward. It granted you one final moment of lucidity, enabling you to stand up from the table and drop down again onto the nearest couch.

In a sticky voice, Boutros insisted that I lie down next to him. I fought against the torpor; I shrank, not daring actually to leave the bed but avoiding touching his body. When he began to snore, I turned over onto my back and gazed around the room to pass the time. In the dim light the room seemed to be spinning: the low ceiling; the mauve flowers; the dusty furniture littered with knickknacks and more dust. The room went around and around, never changing, merging this first day with those still to come. It was a turning orb with no exit, this room that was spinning, tracing circles as its image pressed against my temples.

*   *   *

I would have to get accustomed to this room.

The days to come seemed to be lined up before my door with faces as pale as those of schoolgirls waiting in line. How could I free myself from their monotonous faces and infuse them with a little warmth? In spite of everything, I thought about this with such concentration that the desire to live renewed my energy.

I wanted to recreate my room by rearranging the furniture, getting rid of the artificial flowers in their earthenware jug and the other odds and ends. I dusted the chairs, dreaming of gay-colored material to brighten them up. I thought of Om el Kher, with her mingled scents of earth and henna. "I don't mean to offend you," she had said, "but what good will it do you to know how to read and write?" I would teach the little ones in the village how to read, the big ones as well. I saw myself as mothers see their children, as part of myself and yet as someone separate and unique.

When Abou Sliman came back to prepare dinner, I was almost happy. "Listen," I said, "before you start, go and bring me flowers. Go and cut branches. Bring back as many as you can."

He returned with his arms heaped high and I filled all the glasses, bottles and vases I could find with flowering branches.

Abou Sliman appeared in the doorway holding a half-plucked chicken. He was smiling: "How beautiful, all these branches!" he exclaimed. "How beautiful! I would never have thought of it myself." He went off, holding the chicken at arm's length, but he turned around again to say: "How beautiful! A person would think he was out in the fields." Then he disappeared. I heard the stove crackling, and the smell of cooking food spread through the house.

I had taken down the velvet draperies at the entrance. I hated their touch. I had opened the windows. The light played upon the walls, on the bare furniture and on the flowering branches. From time to time Abou Sliman's head bobbed in through the half-open door; he had the same smile.

The room was becoming my room.

Toward the end of the afternoon Boutros arrived. He kissed me on the forehead:

"I have found the culprit," he said.

"The culprit?"

But suddenly he pushed me aside so he could take in the changes in the house. His eyes popped wide open. He yelled at Abou Sliman, who came running, his apron stained with chicken feathers.

"Son of a bitch!" Boutros shouted. "What have you done to my house?"

I stepped back to explain: "It wasn't Abou Sliman. It was me. I did it all."

Boutros paid no attention to my words. "Is this an insult to me and Sit Rachida, you good-for-nothing!"

"But Boutros Bey . . ."

Boutros lifted his arm as if he were about to hit Abou Sliman. I begged Boutros to listen to me; I kept repeating that Abou Sliman was not responsible.

"You!" he exclaimed. "Get back to your room. This is my affair! Don't interfere!"

I went to my room; my legs were shaking.

"Close the door behind you," Boutros shouted.

His voice kept rising, punctuated by the cook's thin treble: "But Boutros Bey . . ."

I held my ear to the door.

"Put everything back as it was, and hurry up!" Boutros ordered. "Where are my things? Where are they, you thief, you son-of-a-thief? And the velvet curtains? The artificial flowers? Have you ever seen branches in a house before? Throw these branches out, you good-for-nothing!"

I heard doors opening and things being put back where they had been before.

"No, not there, not there," Boutros was saying. "The tower goes more to the right, next to the ivory elephant."

This was the gilded bronze tower I had put away in the bottom of a drawer. I heard the water being poured out of the vases and then the dry rustling of the artificial flowers.

"The flowers my sister gave me," said Boutros. "They never die. They don't need water. They are eternal. Do you hear? You threw them away, you son-of-a-bitch!"

Abou Sliman protested no longer. He was hanging up the velvet draperies on their rusty rings. My room was no longer my room. It was replaced by that other stale-smelling room.

And I was not like those artificial flowers that can live without water. I was fragile; the dryness would kill me.

I kept my ear to the door while the room was deformed, while Abou Sliman was insulted and abused because of my actions, and while Boutros, already seated in his green chair, twirled his amber beads, waiting for the moment when he could sit down at the dinner table.

* * *

"So," Boutros resumed, "I was telling you I found the culprit."

We were seated at the round table. Abou Sliman was serving the dishes. I didn't dare look at him.

"I went to the village," Boutros went on. "Nobody wanted to talk. Nobody would tell me who had been singing. I was sure they all knew. I questioned the blind man; he did not tell me anything either. And he knew! The blind man knows everything. Women tell him their secrets. So I threatened them all. I told them I would bring in girls from other villages to do the harvesting. And I left. Bahia ran after me in tears. She kept repeating, 'It was me.' She is Abou Sliman's niece. A bad lot. Her father taught her a lesson though, in front of me!"

I hated Boutros. Hatred made my disgust swell. I saw him and all the Boutros's in the world in their rigid authoritarianism. They ruled over destinies; they crushed plants, songs, colors, they crushed life itself. And they reduced everything to the shriveled proportions of their own hearts. All these Boutros's advancing! But a day would come....

Boutros was eating, smacking his lips. Abou Sliman cleared the table and lit the lamp. A day would come when the muffled fires that encircled the Boutros's of the world would give way to roaring flames. A day would come, perhaps, when our daughters would no longer be like moss growing around the trunks of dead trees. Our daughters would be different. They would throw off this torpor, the sleepwalker's state that engulfed me whenever I heard the voice of this man.

"This Bahia has already given me trouble. But a good beating is never without effect. Why don't you answer me? Well, you're right. It's my business, after all. Never interfere!"

Abou Sliman took away the white tablecloth and replaced it with another woven of silk. He placed the lamp in the center of the table, turned it up as far as it would go, then he left, returning with two dog-eared packs of cards.

"Do you know how to play?"

"No."

"Then watch me. It's called 'Solitaire.' "

The lamp crackled, giving off a raw glare that was almost unbearable. Boutros laid down the cards, one after another. "Red over black," he explained. "You see, it's easy, and it makes the time go by. I play Solitaire every evening."

His amber beads, still warm from the touch of his fingers, were resting near his elbow. "Give me the Jack of Clubs. I really believe this will work out."

Abou Sliman brought the coffee. Boutros sipped it noisily. When he put down his cup a dark trail ran around his lips.

"This time I really feel it will succeed," he went on.

I sat tamely at his side and handed him the cards he asked for. I submitted to boredom.

"No, no," Boutros said, "I want the Queen of Diamonds. Don't you see, red over black. Black over red. Spades, Clubs, Hearts. . . ."

My life was crumbling away at this table, with the game of Solitaire. Day after day it was leaving me. I was wilting. I was not at all like the immortal paper flowers!

"I've won! I've won!" Boutros cried. "I knew it! Pick up the cards. We are going to start all over again!"

*   *   *

6 The first month went by slowly. During the day I watched Abou Sliman carry his feather duster limply, like an unwanted object attached to his wrist. Around Abou Sliman there was a tissue woven of habits inside of which he moved with an absent air and a rough and tragic expression. In his face was incarnated all the sadness in the world. His eyes did not seem to belong to him. I did not talk to him any more. I hardly dared to approach him. Often, when I heard his steps, I would go into the next room. I was certain he was angry at me because of the scene Boutros had made and the reprimands, which were my fault.

Om el Kher came every other day with her daughter Zeinab, carrying a basket of fruits and vegetables. She greeted me deferentially and always wished me a blessed day. Om el Kher rapidly enumerated the produce she had brought, blessed me once again and disappeared immediately, followed by Zeinab, who never opened her mouth. Them also; I had lost them too. And Bahia? Bahia who no longer sang under my windows.

All this made it impossible for me to visit the village. Nonetheless, I wanted to do it. And I wanted to meet the blind man Boutros had mentioned. One morning, tired of ambling about between my four walls, I decided to go for a walk in the countryside. I took the path that led away from the village, the one which ran straight on toward the horizon.

The sky was low, like a ceiling weighed down by the opaque sun. I hurried along, feeling lonelier than ever because of the hatred that I imagined was buried in Abou Sliman's heart and in the hearts of Om el Kher and Bahia. I could not forget the humiliations they had endured. I hurried to get away from the village. The path divided the land in two. It was lined with skimpy trees but they provided at least a semblance of shade. The sun burned down upon my head. I went forward, looking straight ahead. Then a voice called:

"Sit! Ya, Sit!"

I turned around and recognized Om el Kher, massive and dark, holding open her arms and beckoning me to come closer. I hesitated a second, then I began to run toward her without asking myself what she wanted. When I was near her, she dropped her arms with an embarrassed air and said:

"Come to the village! I want you to taste my bread!"

Without waiting for an answer, she walked on, leading the way. I felt it had taken all the courage she possessed to call out to me. Now she was walking along without looking at me, seemingly preoccupied with the path. But she soon let out a torrent of words: "I don't want to boast, but my bread is the best bread in the village! 'Om el Kher's bread!' " She turned around and laughed, a short nervous laugh: " 'Om el Kher's bread,' " she went on, "that's what everyone calls it. I want you to taste it. Did the Bey enjoy the watermelon I brought yesterday? I cut into it with a knife to make sure it was really ripe. Look," she said, turning to me again, "this tree is a mango tree. When the fruit ripens, I'll bring you some. If you want to know if a mango is ready to eat, you must feel its belly. It must be neither too soft nor too hard, like the belly of a newborn baby."

I liked to hear Om el Kher talk. I liked her gestures. When I was near her, I felt sheltered.

"You are wearing the blue stone, I see," she said, glancing at my blouse. I did not believe in the power of beads, but nevertheless, I would never be without this stone again. "You'll have a son," she went on, "as sure as I'm looking at you now. You'll have a son."

The village stood behind a row of greenery not far from the avenue of young banana trees. Their wild branches, tied up in rags, made them look like girls with woolly hair piled on top of their heads. "Your son will grow up along with these banana trees," said Om el Kher. "By the time he is three, he'll be eating their fruit!"

Here was the village; it looked like a mud cake. Not a single door opened onto the countryside. All looked inward onto a dusty narrow street. The roofs were covered with all kinds of debris, straw, tin and other odds and ends.

"I have been watching you for a long time," said Om el Kher. "Your visit is an honor for the village."

"You know," I answered, "I have wanted to come for a long time, but after the Bey got angry, I was afraid that . . ."

"Yes, yes," said Om el Kher and she walked faster. My explanation made her uncomfortable. "Yes, I know. You had lots to do at home. You must take your time. All the women here have been wanting to see you. They have been talking about it with the blind man. But I told them they must be patient."

The houses were attached to one another and ragged children were hanging about the doorways. The women, crouched on the ground or standing around, were calling out to each other, and their words seemed like cries. When they caught sight of me, they stopped.

"At this time of day," Om el Kher said, "the men are all in the fields. The village belongs to the children, to the women and to the blind man."

* * *

Om el Kher's tumbledown house was at one end of the village; we had to walk past all the others to reach it. Since I had arrived, the women had stopped talking; they stood around, open-mouthed, nudging each other in the ribs. Flies were buzzing around the children, clinging to their shirts. The women's eyes were fixed on my dress, my hair, my breasts, my belly. They were probably wondering if I was already carrying a child. They did not like barren women.

"This is Nefissa," said Om el Kher stopping before an old woman who was sitting on the ground drawing lines and circles in the sand with her finger. "She predicts the future. But nothing she predicts ever comes true. Isn't that so, Nefissa, my beauty?"

"You're a crazy old woman!" snapped Nefissa. "Crazy, and an unbeliever too. An unbeliever!"

"Me?" protested Om el Kher with her hands on her hips. She believed in Allah, she said. "She believed in the Sheikha, the Sheikha who *truly* knew the future. I'll take you to the Sheikha whenever you want," she told me. Then, addressing Nefissa again, she added, "So, Nefissa, don't call me a crazy old woman! Do you hear! Don't ever call me a crazy old woman again. You are twice my age. You could be my grand-mother!"

I could sense the enjoyment they took in bickering.

"Her grandmother!" exclaimed Nefissa. "No, just look at her, this bag of rags! Her face looks like every hand on earth kneaded it!" She laughed. "And ugly, on top of it all! The old bat!"

They were both laughing now. Om el Kher was crouched beside her friend. She tapped her on the back; their faces were close together.

"Old scarecrow!"

"Rusty old can!"

"Listen," said Nefissa. "Since this is the first time the lady has come to the village, let me tell her fortune."

"No, no, Nefissa, not today. Another time. Today she has come to the village to taste my bread."

"Your bread! Your bread! You mean your grains of sand!"

This time, however, Om el Kher was angry. Her nostrils flared; she frowned.

"Bread of sand! Bread of straw! Bread of drudgery!" sang out Nefissa.

"The grandmothers are fighting again," someone yelled.

"Be quiet," scolded another voice, but not unkindly. "Aren't you ashamed. It's obvious that the men are in the fields."

"Come, let's go," said Om el Kher, beckoning to me.

Nefissa lifted her fat creased face toward us. "May life be good to you! As good as the bread of Om el Kher. The best in all the village."

Om el Kher smiled at her then, and turning to me, said: "Follow me." After a while she stopped again: "Nefissa is pure gold. I have known her all my life. But when you want to hear what the future has in store for you, I'll take you to the Sheikha. She lives in the neighboring village. But it is well worth going that far to hear her."

* * *

I was still following Om el Kher. "It's over there, the last door," she assured me.

A woman had been watching us for a few minutes. Like ivy, she seemed attached to the wall against which she was leaning. Her young face, like her surroundings, was sad and muddy. Her eyes were motionless, but open; she seemed only half-awake.

"Ratiba! Ratiba!" called Om el Kher as we passed her. "Come and greet the Bey's wife!"

Ratiba made an effort to detach herself from the wall; she took a few wobbly steps in our direction. "May your days be happy," she said and a vague smile flickered about her mouth.

"Come, come," said Om el Kher. "With time things improve. They get to be forgotten. It's no use thinking about the past all the time."

"I hate them!" said Ratiba. "I hate them!"

I could see her teeth gleaming. It was as if she forced her words through them. Then she closed her lips tightly and stared rigidly ahead.

"You spend all your time going over the same things," said Om el Kher. "You must forget. What good is it to keep remembering?"

"I hate them," hissed Ratiba. "I hope they die! I hope they hang, both of them!"

"Be quiet, what if the men hear you?"

"I don't care. They must die! I'll say it again, they must die!"

She spoke as if I didn't exist. Her tragedy clung to her like a second skin. My presence, which awoke in the others a childlike curiosity, left her completely indifferent. She moved away from us, walking backward. When she felt the wall at her back, she leaned against it, sighing deeply.

"She is going mad," said Om el Kher. "Maybe she is already mad. She is the sister of Sayyeda."

"Sayyeda?"

"Yes." Om el Kher spoke in a mysterious tone. "Everyone knows about Sayyeda. Even the papers wrote about it."

For a second I wanted to stop Om el Kher from telling the story. I felt that Ratiba's grief would cling to me forever. The suffering of others smothered me; hers would do so as well. But Om el Kher went on. She told me what had happened to Sayyeda. Her father and brother had stabbed her to death. She was the oldest and had brought up all the children. She had brought up Ratiba, too. One evening someone saw Sayyeda near the palm grove with a man. Her father and brother found out about it. She was a widow, Sayyeda, but to be seen with a man cast shame upon her. The father and the brother lost their heads. They killed her. "But Ratiba loves her sister too much. She doesn't make allowances. She forgets that her father and her brother were right in a way. In all the villages the men approved of the murder. It was an affair of honor. The men, above all, approved of it. The women took it as a warning. But Ratiba does not want to understand. Her father and her brother are in hiding. She wants them found and killed. She is going mad!"

Om el Kher was speaking fast, as if this were better forgotten. "At my age," she said, "I could tell you many tales. But I want to forget them. It is quite the opposite for some people. If they don't have stories of their own, they live on other people's. Sayyeda's tragedy belongs to the village now. This prevents Ratiba from forgetting."

How can one help Ratiba? And what sort of help could possibly be enough? The world had to change. This world of illusion which was imposed upon us as if it were really life.

With confusion I sensed this. But who could I talk to about it?

A child grasped my skirt. Except for a tuft of hair above his forehead, his head was shaved. "A millieme, give me a millieme," he begged, "just one!"

"Child of sin!" cried Om el Kher. "Go back to your mother who teaches you to beg!"

Other women were following us. They stood close to one another, so close that their robes seemed to form a single garment. I was struck by one of them, by her lucid expression and her fluttering eyelids. She seemed to embody all the laughter of the village. It was difficult not to smile when she came forward, her fat body shaking. She used her ugliness as one shakes a rattle at a child, for amusement. "You are going to try Om el Kher's bread," she said. "It is the best bread in the village. I don't make bread any longer. My arms are too fat. I can hardly move them now!" And she started beating her arms against her hips as if she were desperately trying to lift them to her shoulders, then she let them fall heavily, giving out great bursts of laughter.

"Her name is Salma," said Om el Kher. "Salma can make you forget anything. She can take your sorrows and shake them as through a large sieve until nothing remains but fine dust which she blows away on the winds. Only Ratiba never laughs. She stands in the same place and lets the sun beat down on her. Salma makes everybody laugh," said Om el Kher. "She can make even the blind man laugh."

I often heard the blind man mentioned. To me he seemed like some sort of silent divinity who reigned over the village when the men were away.

"Often," went on Om el Kher, "Salma makes the blind man laugh. Except when he is cross. Nobody can forget the days when the blind man gets cross! The day Bahia was beaten, he got angry." But Om el Kher excused him, saying, "It is such a long time since he saw anything. He lives in another world. "

When his anger rises, he beats the ground with his stick. Ten years ago a woman from this village stole fourteen artichokes and thirty kilos of beans from the storehouse. The old

manager, the one before the Bey, your husband, came with
police officers. They took the woman away and she was sen-
tenced to five years in prison. She said she had seven children and that she couldn't bear to hear them cry of hunger
any longer. But they took her away."

"It was wrong to steal. We were all frightened. We all
stayed closed up in our houses. But the blind man refused to
move. Maybe because he couldn't see he wasn't as frightened
as the rest of us. He stayed in the middle of the street while
they took the woman away. We were all in our houses but
he was alone in the middle of the street. He was beating the
ground with his stick, pounding with all his strength."

"You can't imagine the strength of a blind man! Because
he doesn't waste it looking around, he keeps it locked up
inside himself and sometimes it explodes. The blind man was
standing there and he was beating the ground with all his
might. He ended up making a hole in the ground in which
to bury his anger. We all watched him from behind our
half-closed doors. The children climbed up on one another's
shoulders to get a look at him through the windows. He was
alone in the street, beating the ground with his stick. It
lasted a long time, long after the woman was taken away.
When we came out of our houses, he had stopped. And those
who went near him saw that he was weeping."

"Here is my house," said Om el Kher, without stopping to
take a breath.

*   *   *

Brown smoke was coming out the door. Om el Kher told
me to wait a minute while she went inside alone. A few
seconds later she handed me a rafia leaf: "Now you can come
in. If the smoke bothers you too much, you can fan yourself."

Inside, Zeinab was seated on the floor with her knees
apart. She was entirely wrapped up in her black robe; one
could see nothing but her toes and her fingers kneading the
dough. She nodded and went on working without taking her
eyes off me.

"Wave the smoke away," said Om el Kher. "It's a nuisance
when you're not used to it."

They weren't at all bothered by the smoke. She sat on the floor and picked up some brown dough, fashioned it into a ball, threw it from one hand to another, and then she bounced the dough up and down on a long-handled wooden paddle until it spread out like a flat sheet which she slid slowly off the paddle into the oven. Now and then she took a handful of twigs and threw them on the fire. The top of the clay oven served as a bed at night. The smoke filled the room, making our faces sooty; I coughed to clear my throat.

As she drew out the first round loaf of bread from the oven, Om el Kher said: "It is as rounded as goat's skin and as light as the summer breeze. Taste it. You will like it."

The bread was like a golden balloon which collapsed when I bit into it. I enjoyed the acrid taste.

"Well?" said Om el Kher.

"Well?" said Zeinab.

My mouth was so full I couldn't answer.

"Eat, eat all of it!" they said. "We'll give you another loaf to take home."

They opened the oven door. The fire sparkled, making our faces glow. The two women drew out the warm fresh bread and filled my arms with it, loading me down with bread. The flour turned my dress white. When I could hold no more, Om el Kher said: "I'll go with you to carry the rest. That way, you'll have enough for two or three days."

It was then, with my arms full of bread, that I met the blind man. I was carrying too much. Stumbling on a stone, I lost my balance. The bread fell to the ground. I was able to hold onto only one loaf, which I clutched to my chest with my nails dug into its soft side. At first I saw only his back. He was bent over, helping me pick up the bread. But I knew it was the blind man. At this hour there was no other man in the village. He was comforting Om el Kher.

"It doesn't matter," he said. "Dust won't stick to it." He took two or three loaves in his hands and rubbed them on the front of his robe before handing them back to me. I repeated "Thank you." I felt clumsy and awkward. Om el Kher looked like a child who had been beaten.

"It doesn't matter, Om el Kher," said the blind man again. "A bit of dust won't harm bread like yours."

Then he smiled and turned to me, adding: "Your visit is
a great joy for the village." His smile was so brilliant it took
the place of his eyes. He had a delicately formed chin, transparent nostrils, and he was wearing a large very white turban which seemed freshly laundered.

I repeated "Thank you." I could find nothing else to say
before following Om el Kher, who had partly recovered.

*   *   *

On the way home I thought about the blind man. I would
like to have stayed with him a little longer. Having listened
to others so much, he probably knew what went on in their
hearts. "The blind man knows everything," Boutros had
said. "The women tell him their secrets."

I thought about the blind man. I associated him with the
earth, dark and wise, that makes all things swell and grow.
"He was standing upright, beating the ground," Om el Kher
had said. "He ended up making a huge hole in the earth."

I thought of nothing else on the way back. I imagined him
going forth with slow deliberate footsteps as though he were
bearing the fate of the village. With his large white turban
which shone like a jewel, a crown of linen, and his smooth
face, he seemed like a king. "At this hour," said Om el Kher,
"the village belongs to the children, to the women and to the
blind man."

She looked back to see whether I was following, then
crossed the threshold and preceded me up the stairs. The
door was ajar; Boutros had already returned.

In the kitchen Om el Kher helped me put the bread in the
wicker basket under the table before slipping away noise-
lessly.

In the living-room, pounding the arms of his chair with his
fists, Boutros growled: "No more going to the village alone.
You must maintain your position. One does not mix with the
common women. Rachida never set foot in the village. They
brought everything she needed to the house. She knew how
to keep her distance." He went on, his eyebrows rising as he

scowled. "The wife of a Nazer does not hang around the village. It is no place for a respectable woman!"

I didn't know what to answer. He got up, walked toward the kitchen, bent over, pulled the basket from under the table, and lifted the clean cloth that covered the bread.

"This bread! I don't want it. These women have dirty hands. I have my bread brought from the nearest town. There is a bakery there. I will not eat this bread. It can give one all sorts of diseases. Throw it away! It's fit only for animals."

7 Time passed. I allowed it to pass. The mirror attached to the coatstand in the entrance hall confronted me brutally with the past eight years. I was only twenty-four, but what meaning is there in numbers? When I glanced at my face by accident I at first wanted to flee, then I came closer and looked at it. My eyelids were puffy. A layer of dull fat had settled around my chin. My cheeks had lost their color, and rouge went on badly, in two powdery spots. When I ran my fingertips over my skin, I seemed to hear the sound of paper rustling. There were two lines around my mouth. My expression was rigid and troubled. I pulled back my hair with a purple band so I wouldn't feel its dryness on my temples.

When I stepped back a little the mirror framed me from the waist up. My figure was heavy. When I placed my hands on my hips I had the impression of tired flesh under my palms; when I crossed them on my belly, which had never carried a child, it felt heavy and numb. With each step I took the loose heel of my slipper hit the floor with a dull thud.

I hated my own image. I was something other than that. I knew this well. In my arms there were other arms, behind my eyes, other eyes, and inside of me there was another me, whom I held prisoner and who rebelled against this slow death toward which I was leading her.

How much I now resembled the other women of my country! Their shoulders rounded and their lives torn to shreds by routine! But whereas they were resigned, I did not accept my life. My human life could not be this, only this. I refused to accept it, neither for them nor for myself, neither for the poor nor for the rich. I refused to believe that for the women of my country, as the common idea went, money was a compensation for solitude. No one ever looked at these women with the sort of love that can transform life. What power has money, compared to love? I didn't accept my life but I didn't know what to do or where to turn.

I wanted to discover, reflected in a pair of loving eyes, the image of the woman I could have been, but I had only this mirror with its icy surface under my hands; every day Abou Sliman polished it to a shine.

* * *

I was alone. My family? I hardly ever heard from them. My brothers were married now; their wives took it for granted that I was lost to the life of the city. They didn't seem to have much trouble forgetting me. My father had visited Boutros and me twice. On one of these visits he told me that Zariffa had died.

Each time my father came we killed a lamb.

His business seemed prosperous but he always complained about it, for fear I should ask for money. I had no intention of doing so in spite of Boutros, who was always after me: "He gave you no dowry. I have always had to bear the expenses. His business is doing well. He's just bought a new car! People say your sisters-in-law are covered with jewelry! Don't put up with it. You must demand something!"

My father talked; he said: "You must have a child." He said: "Times are hard!" He said: "Ah! Country air! There's nothing like country air for good health! You are lucky." Then, early in the afternoon, he left.

"Well?" Boutros asked as soon as the car had disappeared around the bend of the avenue of banana trees. His arm was still raised to say goodbye to my father, who was waving his white handkerchief.

"Well?"

I ran up the staircase without answering.

*   *   *

I had never returned to the village.

The women seemed to understand that I had to "maintain my position," but an uneasiness settled between us for a different reason. I was barren and they didn't trust barren women. At first they questioned me: "Will it be a boy for our Bey?" Then they got discouraged and tried to avoid me. There was pity in Om el Kher's voice. And Boutros said: "I have received a letter from Rachida. She says this is not natural. They deceived us about your health. That's what she says!"

This child, I wished for it now. I constantly breathed this longing, whispering it to the plants, to the night and to the sun. I was filled with shame and anguish. To try to divert myself I walked in the countryside. How solemn and indifferent the land was! Yet it soothed me, the low houses, the trees and the river banks whose pale colors mingled together before flowing into the yellowish waters of the canal. Sometimes a sail appeared in the distance, a boat going who knew where. A sail erect, alive above the banks of weeping willows.

Boutros said: "Amin, the head of the village, has just repudiated his wife. After two years of marriage she has given him no children. As for me, my religion forbids me to do so!" And he crossed himself.

I tried to forget the sound of his voice. I watched the women moving with long firm steps, balancing jars on their heads. At the banks of the river they fastened their skirts up around their waists and began washing clothes. Around them water buffaloes were bathing, nothing but their black muzzles visible above the water.

"Gamalat, Hussein's wife, has borne only girls," Boutros said. "It looks like a punishment sent from heaven!"

It was not to silence Boutros that I yearned for a child. It was a true longing, and it never left me. I carried this dream with me everywhere. Whenever I heard children's voices I would lean over the balcony railing, listening to their stories and their laughter as they played in the narrow alley below. I followed their motions, admiring the roundness of their arms and the smoothness of their wrists. I would have liked to invite them upstairs so I could get to know them better, and in spite of the dust in the folds of their plump necks and the flies on their eyelids, I longed to press them to me and to talk to them.

One morning when it was much colder than usual I decided to go for a walk and I took from the armoire a coat my father had given me; it had been his coat. "You can have it remade for yourself," he had said, "it's good enough for the country." I had not had it remodeled. It just hung in the armoire with my other clothes, all of which needed attention, a stitch or a button.

When it was cold outdoors the house seemed freezing; the doors and windows let the wind pass through, and the cold settled, clinging to the walls and to the doorknobs. Often, I stayed curled up for hours, just waiting for the time to come when I could go to bed with a hot water bottle under the covers.

On this particular morning I put on my father's old coat before going out; it gave me drooping shoulders and hung to my ankles. The wind rushed through the sleeves. To warm up I walked quickly. I wanted only to walk, to think of nothing except how to keep my legs moving. To chase away thoughts, I started counting. Numbers had the power to chase away my anguish for a time: One. Two. Three. I counted my steps. Fifteen. Sixteen. Seventeen. My mind was busy. I must go on counting. I felt warmer. A kind of joy seized me, the feeling of being nothing more than a body walking. Eighty-three. Eighty-four. . . .

I was already far from the village when I heard footsteps behind me. Someone was following me. Voices, low and mysterious, were coming nearer, the voices of children. They seemed to be talking about me.

"This time she must be!" said one voice.

But another contradicted this statement at once. No, it was impossible now.

"But I tell you, she is!" the first child insisted.

I heard snatches of conversation and the pattering of their feet on the ground.

"I bet you!"

"What do you bet?"

"My red ball."

"The one you found on the road near the river?"

"Yes."

"I want it!"

But the one who had wagered his ball was obstinate. He would yield it only to the child who was bold enough to look.

"I tell you she is! We must go and see!"

"And if there is nothing?"

"You get the red ball."

"It will be mine!" returned the challenger.

"No, mine!" And they started quarreling.

I wanted to walk faster, to take a side path and to escape. But I felt a hand clutch at my coat, then another. The children encircled me. They pushed against one another, without looking up at me. One of them seized my coat roughly and pulled it open, amidst their shouts.

The red ball was lost! Its owner ran off through the fields, followed by the others.

I sat down on a stone at the edge of the path; my arms were dangling like inert objects. I no longer felt the cold. The children's mockery resounded in my head; I could think of nothing else. For a long time I did not move. Then I felt a hand slip into mine, a hand that felt as warm as a bird's breast.

"My name is Ammal," said the little girl.

She had two thin braids, reddish in color, tied on top of her head. I couldn't tell whether her eyes were smiling or sad because they seemed drowned in a kind of misty look that made her expression indistinct.

"I want to go with you," she said. Her words made me want to raise her hand to my lips. But I didn't want to frighten her. I got up and started walking at her side.

"I know where you live," she said. "I tend the sheep with my uncle Abou Mansour. Every evening we pass under your window."

"How old are you?"

"I don't know. My mother doesn't know either. But I am still little."

"I think you are five."

"Five!" Ammal added, "I'll tell my brothers tonight."

"Do you have many brothers?"

"I have only brothers," she answered. As we reached the house, she added, "This is where you live."

She came with me right to the door, only letting go of my hand at the bottom step. "Go on up," she said to me.

"Come and see me again, Ammal. I'll make you a dress."

She had very white teeth which shone when she smiled. She threw her head back and watched me climb. Her expression was confident and her gaze never left me. At each step, I turned around to wave to her.

"Come back, Ammal!"

She was at the bottom of the staircase, holding on to the knob of the railing. She craned her neck, and I leaned over to smile at her one last time.

*　*　*

And then it was over. Ammal's face eluded me as soon as the door was closed.

The comfort she had brought disappeared with her presence. In my room there was no escape; even the objects seemed deformed. They were no longer chairs, tables, lamps and carpets; they took on monstrous shapes. The colors lost their brightness, and everything showed signs of decay. The threads of the curtains were worn thin, eaten by the sun and the dust. The ceiling was low; the walls were closing in on me. I could have screamed.

A friendly face would have banished this nightmare. I believed in the unlimited powers of a friendly face, but it was impossible for me to recover one from the depths of my sluggish mind. I wished for Om el Kher's face, or that of Zariffa—dead now—for the face of my dead mother, or for that of Ammal, whom I had just left. Their names were no more substantial than words blowing in

the wind; they evoked nothing. I yearned to go to sleep.
Ceaselessly, I waited for night and for the midday siesta,
which had become a habit with me, and then, again, I waited
for night.

Somebody knocked at the door, or rather, scratched on it.

"May I come in?" asked a voice I hardly recognized. "Can
I speak to you?"

It was Om el Kher. Hesitantly, she entered as if burdened
with a secret. "Listen," she burst out bluntly. "The children
saw you today, and they told what they saw. They have been
talking about you in the village. I can't stand it anymore. It
makes my heart ache." Her voice thickened, as if it were
rolled in earth. "Maybe it isn't my business, but I don't like
to hear such things. You have no children, and you are pining away. Every morning when I bring my basket I see, I
have eyes, but I don't say anything. I tell Zeinab alone: 'The
Bey's wife is pining away because she is barren.' Do you
remember Nefissa, the old chatterbox who reads fortunes in
the sand?"

"Yes, I remember."

"I have consulted her. She says you must go and see the
Sheikha."

"Who is the Sheikha?"

"I told you about her the day you came to taste my bread.
You must see the Sheikha. She will tell you what to do."

"But who is she?" I repeated.

"Everybody knows who the Sheikha is," and Om el Kher
started telling me her tale. Very quickly, as she always
talked, without taking time to catch her breath, she explained: "When Sheikha Raghia died, the neighboring village, all the neighboring villages, in fact, went into
mourning."

I was sitting on the edge of the sofa while Om el Kher
squatted nearby on the floor. She saw that the sun was still
high and, knowing that she had plenty of time before Boutros returned, she continued: "It was Sheikha Raghia who
cured the sick and brought back unfaithful husbands. It was
she who helped to find thieves and stolen goods. She had
powders. You know, powders a person burns. She also had
bits of paper on which she wrote words she alone understood.

Sheikha Raghia could help a girl find a husband and conceive a child. Women told her their troubles. She chased away devils! When she died people thought all kinds of misfortunes would befall them, and for a whole month illness and grief seemed to be everywhere. Husbands abandoned their wives. And then one day, in the street of the "Obstinate One," Bayumi who sold lemonade—he was only a very young man at the time—all of a sudden Bayumi was seized by a fit of trembling. He fell to the ground. Perspiration stood out on his skin. He gasped. A strange voice came from his throat. Somebody who was passing by recognized Sheikha Raghia's voice. If only you had heard her scream! Others came running and they, too, recognized the voice of Sheikha Raghia. Bayumi was carried to the Shiekha's house. You see, Sheikha Raghia had chosen Bayumi, and she inhabited his body. So the women called Bayumi "Blessed One," and for the last thirty years, the Sheikha has inhabited Bayumi and has gone on helping us. Some day I'll tell you what she did for me. And you, you are getting on in years," Om el Kher went on, "And when you have not borne a son, years count twice as much. The Bey will be away all day tomorrow, I have been told. I have spoken to Abou Sliman. He'll drive the Bey to the station and when he gets back, the car will be ours."

I had no faith in the powers of the Sheikha, but I was happy at the thought of spending the day with Om el Kher.

"Tomorrow then," she said, "May Allah bless you!"

"Tomorrow," said Boutros before getting into bed, "I shall be away all day. Tell Abou Sliman to kill two pigeons and roast them for my dinner."

* * *

At the end of the Street of the Obstinate One in a cul-de-sac named "The Prophetess" a staircase as narrow as a ladder rose between the flanks of two cracked walls.

"We have reached your holy house at last, oh Holy One!" exclaimed Om el Kher. "These stairs are cruel that keep me away from you. If only I could live in your shadow forever, oh Blessed One!" To climb the stairs, she raised the muddy hem of her robe above her ankles. "This is it!" she cried out, her voice elated.

The stairway opened onto a moon-shaped passage. A few broken steps. Another dark corridor, then the open sky. On the roof was a cluster of rooms. Again, Om el Kher started talking of "this blessed house," and when she turned toward me, pointing at one of the open doors, I saw that she was smiling. "Listen!" Om el Kher insisted, stopping short, "she is talking!"

An effeminate voice could be heard, dropping words one by one, and halting between sentences as if waiting for the next to be dictated.

"Your fig tree bears nothing but thorns," said the voice. "However much you care for it, you will only prick your fingers! But listen carefully, in the space of three intervals you will find the fig. It will be hidden; you will have to search for a long time. But when the day comes, I'll rejoice with you. I will wear a rose above my ear!"

The voice was silent.

"We can go in now," said Om el Kher, making me pass before her.

The room was spacious. Against the walls strange objects were piled up, gifts to the Sheikha: pigeon cages resting against the carved black furniture; a stuffed gazelle precariously balanced on top of a lacquered armoire; a wooden tower resembling a toy filled with multicolored feathered flowers. The pieces of a broken vase lay on the floor next to an oil jar. Several drawers overflowed with silk scarves, glass necklaces, a watch chain, and assorted glass beads. On the far wall a large painting portrayed a Holy Man standing under a tree; the painting was half hidden by a potted palm in a large earthenware pot.

Om el Kher whispered into my ear that the Sheikha had painted the picture. "The trees look so real," she asserted, "that sometimes birds fly into the room and try to nest in them."

The Sheikha was speaking again and Om el Kher and I were still standing near the door. Nobody had noticed us. I could see the Sheikha from behind, sitting on a low couch surrounded by crouching women who formed a great flowing mass of black at her feet.

Still other objects were heaped up on shaky tiers of shelves, on window ledges, on the lacquered furniture, on the floor. Animals were moving about freely. A goat and its kid, a dog, a hen with almost no feathers, a turkey cock. They came and went among the empty boxes, the abundance of watering cans and the old clothes; sometimes the animals brushed against the women's robes.

The Sheikha stopped talking and turned around suddenly. She recognized Om el Kher and lifted both hands, swinging them to and fro in a gesture of welcome.

"Greetings, Om el Kher! So it's you, my old friend! I have missed you!" Then the Sheikha winked. "What misfortune brings you here, my old friend? What misfortune?" she repeated.

Overwhelmed by this attention, Om el Kher put her hands to her lips in a gesture of gratitude. "Sheikha," she said, "it's not for me. It's for the lady with me."

The Sheikha beckoned us closer and then she began to cry out in a loud voice: "My wife! My wife, where are you? Bring a chair for the lady."

A fat woman wearing a white sack-like shirt that reached to her ankles came into the room. Her hands were dripping with soap suds; she had been washing and was annoyed by the interruption. She showed the other women where they would find a stool, and they worked together, struggling to drag it out of a dark corner.

"Closer," said the Sheikha. This privilege embarrassed me, but the others were friendly; and they all smiled at me. "I won't keep you waiting too long. Just give you time to rest," the Sheikha assured me, before addressing Om el Kher, who was already seated with the other women. They rearranged themselves to make room for her.

"Om el Kher, you have lighted up this household! And you are still as vigorous as an old tooth. A trusted molar, my old friend! May Allah bless you!"

Om el Kher beamed. A voice rose from the distant end of the room: "Om el Kher, you have filled the Blessed One's heart with joy. May Allah grant you a long life!"

"Silence," cried the Sheikha. "Silence. Now whose turn is it?"

"It is my turn," said a woman.

"Yes, it's Nabaweyya's turn," echoed the others.

"Well then, Nabaweyya," said the Blessed One, "give me your handkerchief."

Nabaweyya was in the middle of the group. She held out her handkerchief to one of the women, and it was passed from hand to hand. The Sheikha held it to her nose and sniffed it.

The Sheikha was a man of about fifty whose plumpness was emphasized by his white robe. He was seated on a sofa that resembled a washbasin. The Sheikha's face was a round shiny sphere in which his eyes shone like the heads of pins. His nose seemed another ball, a greasy circle above his light moonshaped moustache. His rosy lips looked as if they had been squashing mulberries, and he kept them moist by constantly passing his quick pointed tongue over them. Now and then he puffed on the Turkish water pipe which was bubbling away at his feet. One of the women made sure the pipe was always filled.

The Sheikha's robe had a wide V-shaped neckline which revealed his smooth white chest. Around his neck he wore three necklaces made of jasmine flowers whose odor he sniffed at times, rolling his eyes. When one of the flowers turned yellow, he tore it off his neck and tossed it over his shoulder. On top of his head was a small many-colored cap. People always addressed him as if he were a woman. He was none other than the Sheikha Raghia herself.

I felt at home in this cluttered room. To tell troubles to others and to listen to the troubles of others makes them lighter to bear, and that is sometimes relief enough.

"And so your name is Nabaweyya?" asked the Sheikha, addressing the woman whose handkerchief she had been sniffing.

"Yes."

"Say, 'I hail you, Blessed One.' "

"I hail you, Blessed One."

"The dog you have been caring for has bitten your hand. Its teeth are as sharp as the blade of a kitchen knife. I am going to soften these teeth until they become as soft as tripe, so soft that you will be able to eat them, in turn. Do you understand what I mean, Nabaweyya?"

"Yes, Sheikha."

"Have you any children, Nabaweyya?"

"Yes, Sheikha."

"I knew it."

"May Allah guard them!" cried out the women.

The Sheikha took a sheet of paper from the untidy heap scattered over the sofa; he tore it in two equal parts and started writing on it with a pen whose violet nib he kept moistening with the tip of his tongue, leaving stains at the corners of his mouth. Then he crumpled the paper in his hand, saying, "You will wear this. Wear it between your skin and your chemise. Wear it, and in a week you will find peace again!"

The ball of paper was passed from hand to hand.

"May Allah protect you, Sheikha!" cried Nabaweyya.

"May Allah protect you!" repeated the other women.

Nabaweyya searched for a piaster in the bottom of her pocket.

"This is the first time you have come to me," said the Sheikha. "You can pay some other day."

"I have what is needed, Sheikha," replied Nabaweyya, and she handed him a silver coin.

"As you wish, my sister."

"May Allah shower you with blessings, Oh Beloved One!" cried the women, lavishing good wishes both upon the Sheikha and Nabaweyya.

"Whose turn is it now?" the Sheikha asked.

"Amina's."

"Where are you, Amina?"

"I am here, Blessed one."

She was a young woman with frightened eyes. Her black veil had partly slipped from her head, revealing her gleaming hair. She was waiting close to the sofa near the Sheikha.

"What brings you here, Amina?"

"She has been robbed," answered the others.

"Be quiet, women!" said the Sheikha. "Give me your handkerchief, Amina, and repeat: 'Hail, Blessed One.' "

"Hail, Blessed One!"

"I am listening."

"I have been robbed," repeated Amina, "and if my husband finds out, he will beat me."

"What was stolen?"

"My bracelets. Four gold bracelets, Sheikha. I have been looking for them for the past two days. I have looked everywhere. In corners. In the animals' beds. In my mother-in-law's slippers."

"In your mother-in-law's slippers?"

The woman lowered her head but said nothing.

"Your mother-in-law doesn't like you," went on the Sheikha. "She wants her son to get rid of you."

The woman kept her head lowered. The others were watching her and they began to lament. They gathered even closer together, but the Sheikha began to speak again, reassuring them that things would turn out all right. "You have come from afar but you will not return empty-handed," she told Amina. "You see this powder? I am going to put some in your handkerchief." When Amina's mother-in-law was sleeping, she was to throw a pinch of the powder on her hair. Before the week was over Amina would recover her bracelets. "Your house is as muddy as the sole of a shoe, Amina, but there will be a passageway for you. Do you understand, Amina? A passageway for you."

"Thank you, Sheikha. May Allah repay you!"

"Cast away your fears, Amina. Your life will become as smooth as the flight of a dove, and words will be like honey when they flow toward you."

"Allah bless you, Sheikha. Oh, One Who Sees Everything!"

"No, do not give me anything, Amina. I want nothing from you. You have lost your bracelets. That's more than enough for one week. When you return, bring me a quail. My wife will roast it with some almonds."

"May Allah shower blessings upon you! But at least accept this. Some rose jam. Take it, and may your tongue remain as sweet!" Amina stood up to leave. Her expression had changed. She bent down to stroke the calf, and a joyous impulse made her kiss his nose. As she walked away the Sheikha addressed me:

"It is your turn," she said. "Bring your stool closer."

The women made way. Om el Kher got up to help me.

"Well," resumed the Sheikha when I was settled again, "What can I do to help you?"

"You must help her," put in Om el Kher.

"To begin with, what is your name?"

"Samya."

"Give me your handkerchief, Samya. Say 'Hail, Blessed One.'"

"Hail, Blessed One!"

"What do you wish of me, Samya?"

"She has no children," explained Om el Kher. "No children after eight years of marriage!"

"What a tragedy!" moaned the women. "No children!"

"Be quiet," shouted the Sheikha, "Let me think!" She closed her eyes and wrinkled up her face, concentrating. The women repeated after her, softly, when she began to talk, emphasizing each syllable:

"Samya, Samya. You have an iron knot in your chest. There is a dead bird in your chest, Samya. Maybe your child will bring this bird to life again. You will have a child, Samya. As I see it, a child will come to you."

Om el Kher breathed a sigh of relief, and a great murmur passed through the room as if from a single breast. I myself began to believe that I would have a child.

"For you I shall use three powders," said the Sheikha before opening her eyes.

"You will have a child!" exclaimed the women. "Samya, you will have a child!"

"Women, be quiet! I feel as though a swarm of bees is buzzing around my temples. I am preparing three paper cones, Samya," went on the Blessed One. "In each cone I am putting a different colored powder. You must burn them one after the other in your house. You can go in peace now. May your steps awaken the flowers, Samya!"

I put a few silver coins in the rusty iron box lying at the foot of the sofa. The women gave me their blessings, and as

we left, the Sheikha's gaze followed me as far as the door. On
the way down the stairs we could still hear her voice:

"For you, Zannouba, the moon is clouded over with dust.
In your family someone is on a path which is as black as a
buffalo's back. And I believe it is your son, you unfortunate
one! But in the interval of . . ."

*   *   *

The desire for a child haunted me.

Two years had passed since we had been to see the Sheikha. I had not expected a miracle but I was filled with **8** remorse at the thought that I had perhaps shaken Om el Kher's faith, for she hardly spoke to me anymore, only coming when she was needed. I wondered if she were angry with me. But so few things are inscribed on a face, one never really knows exactly the measure of love or of hatred buried in other people's hearts.

Feelings quickly become entangled. So many barriers exist between human beings, even between those who love each other! When we have finally broken down the walls that surround us, there remain still others, that spring unexpectedly, spontaneously from our inner selves. Each clumsy gesture or oversight contains its own poison which deforms everything it touches. We have to be constantly on the alert, lest we find ourselves locked in separate cages.

Because she is a simple soul, Om el Kher spoke first:

"You must have made a mistake. You probably burned the powders wrong. And that is why you are still childless. But I'll go back and see the Sheikha again. I'll explain it all to her."

"Yes, I must have made a mistake." I knew it was not so; I knew I had thrown away the powders without using them. But I didn't want to say anything that might push Om el Kher farther away from me.

The wish for a child haunted me.

I wanted it for myself. I felt it would open me to life. I also hoped that this birth would bring me closer to the people of the village; I yearned for their sympathy.

As for Boutros, he struck his chest and proclaimed that he was suffering purgatory on earth. He crossed himself, saying: "My faith fortifies me!" At the same time he boasted of having swindled a customer, doubling his own commission. "That fool!" He pursed his lips: "No dowry! No children! If I were not a Christian, I'd throw you out on the street!"

Ammal came to see me. Her uncle Abou Mansour let her bring up the cheese. I called her "my bird," and she came to rub her wings against me, leaving some of her warmth. I had bought a piece of yellow fabric from a peddler to make Ammal a dress. I did not sew well, but I put my heart into the work, and the dress suited her. In all this yellow she looked, I thought, even more like a bird, with her active head and the way she had of fluttering her hands together. I enjoyed watching her, and the yellow dress was so bright that the weakest ray of sun projected the bright color onto the walls. Ammal often sat on the floor with her chin resting on her drawn-up knees, her arms wrapped around her legs, and she would ask me to tell her stories. Just to see the pleasure in her eyes, I found a thousand ideas.

That year for the first time she showed me the little earthen figure she had tucked away in her bodice.

"I made it myself," she said proudly.

The figure represented her uncle Abou Mansour dozing. He was enveloped in sleep and seemed indistinguishable from his robes. His features were barely visible but the likeness was unmistakable; he was just as I had often seen him, resting in the shade of a lime tree. I was filled with joy as I held this small clumsy object. At first I couldn't understand why, but I turned to Ammal and said:

"You will be saved, Ammal!"

I didn't even know what I meant by these words. It was as if I had suddenly understood that Ammal had found an answer to life, and I felt that I must remain at her side to help her.

With her unflinching gaze Ammal penetrated my thoughts.

* * *

The scene with Boutros started unexpectedly.

Once again he was saying: "What good are you if you are not capable of bearing a child?"

I looked him straight in the eye and answered: "And what if it is you?"

"Me? Me?" He stumbled over the words. "Repeat what you just said!"

I put all the rancor I felt in the look I gave him. I wanted to shatter his false dignity.

"Repeat," he said, "Repeat . . ."

"And what if you are the one who is at fault?"

He raised his arm and slapped me. I didn't move. I was glad he had hit me. At last it confirmed this inner brutality which was difficult to define exactly. Until now my hatred had been dispersed among a thousand small actions. Now it took definite shape. What could I have reproached him with before that others would understand? Hadn't he married me without a dowry? Hadn't he been faithful? I was well fed. This is what people saw. The rest was imaginary, they would say, the result of my hysteria!

This time, finally, I could write my father: "Father, this man struck me!"

Before that, what could I have written? "My father, this man treats me like an object? Father, life is passing and I have known no joy? Father, I have never been happy. Father, my days are heavy, and my nights . . . Father, why must I sacrifice happiness if the sacrifice is of no use to anyone? Father, I am thirsty. I yearn to taste water on my lips? Father, with every second that passes, my youth is dying?"

My father would have laughed at a letter containing such thoughts, and then he would have thrown it in the wastebasket.

But this time I could write: "Father, this man hit me! You must come and take me away!"

There were blotches of red on Boutros's forehead and cheeks. He lurched on his small feet, resembling a heap of old clothes ready to collapse. "That is how one must act," he kept repeating. "I have been too kind until now!"

In my letter to my father I would write: "My Father, Boutros beat me. He will do so again. Come and get me quickly!"

"You owe me respect," shouted Boutros. "And you will be dutiful! Do you hear?"

As soon as he receives my letter, my father will come. He will take me away from here. I will go and live with my father.

"One can't stand a madwoman all of one's life! Be careful! I will have you locked up!"

My father's answer was not long in coming. As he had a judicial mind, he took pleasure in collecting the decisions in certain well-publicized lawsuits. He cut one of these out for me, pasted it on a sheet of paper, put it in an envelope, and mailed it. This is what it said: "A man has the right to beat his wife in order to chastise her, but he must not overstep the bounds of the intended castigation."

Then at the bottom of the page in his careful handwriting, he had added: "Do not bring your husband's wrath upon you! Remember, you have often been difficult, even when you were still living at home! Your loving father."

*   *   *

At first, when I realized I was expecting a child, I wanted to keep it a secret. Not to let Boutros know, or Rachida, who would comment at great length in her letters to her brother, on the belatedness of the event. It filled me with an emotion so tender and so deep, this pregnancy, that I wanted to keep away all thoughts that might be harmful to it.

It was Om el Kher I told first, because she was closest to me.

"I knew it," she proclaimed. "The Sheikha is never mistaken!" Then she took a few steps backward, put her hands on her hips and looked me over from head to foot. "So you're a mother now!"

The following days she spoke no more about it, as if she understood that I wanted to surround myself with mystery, but she threw me occasional glances of complicity.

A little later I told Ammal about my condition. At first she cried; she was afraid I would no longer love her as before. I kneeled beside her, telling her over and over again that she was my first little girl and that I would never forget her. I felt a bond between us that was far deeper than words could express.

Ammal was over eight years old now. Her nails were always stained with dirt, her fingers dry as firewood, for she was always busy modeling small figures which she brought to show me.

"When I don't do anything, my fingers burn," she said.

When she spoke of her creations she wore a dreamy smile. "I love them more than my brothers, even more than my uncle Abou Mansour!"

They were nothing much, these little clay objects, but when Ammal spoke of them she seemed to open a whole new world. Ammal would be saved because she possessed a love that could be expressed. A love that could not be extinguished as long as there was blood running in her veins. I could sense this more strongly than she did. To help Ammal, to save her was the only desire that gave meaning to my life. On the evening I told her I was expecting a child, she went away, happy and reassured.

The child in my belly was beginning to show; I couldn't keep it from Boutros any longer:

"It's about time!" he said.

*　*　*

"It will be a son," said Boutros.

I gave a start suddenly, and as if I could touch them, I saw two Boutros's walking toward me, side by side.

I tried to reason with myself, imagining my son as one of the children who played under my windows. Everything seemed to make them laugh: stones, old boards, the mixture of mud and straw which was used as fuel in winter. I tried to imagine my son among the other children, just like them, with black eyes and a merry laugh. At the same time there existed in my mind the image, blown-up and distorted, of

another Boutros walking toward me with the corpulence and
the ridiculous small feet of his father.

At night when I felt oppressed and turned over and over
between the sheets, moaning softly, I could hear their two
voices rising together: Boutros's voice and his son's, both
shouting that I was preventing them from sleeping. Then
they came and stood next to my bed. They had turned on the
lamp, and it gave off a harsh glare through the silk shade.
They were bending over me, both of them together, wearing
identical white cotton nightshirts which reached to their
ankles, unbuttoned at the neck. They had the same thin nose
dividing their sleepy greasy faces right in the middle. Their
shoulders were humped as if they carried bundles on their
backs. Their two shadows fell upon my sheets: "What's the
matter?" they demanded. "You're keeping us from sleeping."

"It will be a son," Boutros said. "I have asked Rachida to
send me a large portrait of St. Theresa. I shall make novenas
one after another until he is born. And a lamp must be kept
burning constantly!"

The portrait arrived in a wooden packing case along with
a supply of flat candles that floated in a glass filled with oil.
It was a large colored portrait in a gilt frame. Boutros had
Abou Sliman nail it to the wall, and a high table for the
candle was placed beneath it.

"You must never let it go out," said Boutros. "You must
watch over it, and you must change the flowers every day!"

I watched over the small flame. I changed the water for the
flowers. The saint had a young girl's face; she soon became
familiar to me, and I performed these boring rituals for her.
As soon as Boutros crossed the doorstep, he went over to the
portrait and stood there mumbling some prayers and striking his chest. I stood behind him, crying out silently: "Let it
be a girl! It must be a girl!" I cried out inwardly, with all my
might struggling to overpower Boutros's prayers. The incessant presence of the flame, however, made me a little un-
easy.

If it should be a girl! She would look like me! Or rather,
like what I wished to be! My daughter would be beautiful! I
would make her strong, humane, and good, with that true

goodness that is so different from the other, that pretended goodness which has the rancid smell of objects that have lain too long in the bottom of a cupboard. But I would be able to mold my daughter as I wished. Confined to these three lifeless rooms, however, would I be able to do this? When these doubts came upon me, I was filled with a desire to run away.

At night I would wake up with a start, covered with sweat. In the interval of a few seconds I lived through one thing, then another. I saw myself picking up my daughter and fleeing. My courage knew no limits; it broke down every obstacle, even my fear, which crumbled like an old stage set. Or else, my head was a mass of tangled questions. Where would I go? I had no money. My father and my brothers would disown me. Nobody would give me work. They would catch me on the road. They might even say I was mad and take my child away from me. Again, I was frozen with fear.

I made one decision. I made another. I was so deeply involved in one that it seemed the alternative had never existed. But then it returned, took charge, and overshadowed the first. There were a thousand reasons to run away and a thousand reasons to remain. The most contradictory thoughts flowed together, and sometimes I wondered, where am I in all of this.

I had not yet resolved this problem when the child was born. It is a perfect word, the word "delivery." Everything sang inside of me. My brain and my heart were reborn. I breathed rhythmically. I seemed to float between layers of air where nothing sharp could touch me. Time had stopped. I was transported to a round green island with a luminous haze surrounding it. A sweet warmth rose to my hips and lingered around my breasts, which seemed light and warm.

Rachida had arrived a few days before the baby was born. "She always answers my call," Boutros had told me. "What devotion! When she gets here, I shall worry no more! She will take charge of everything." Rachida brought three suitcases; she was settling in for a long stay. "She will bring up my son," Boutros had said. "We have the same principles, my sister and I."

At the moment Rachida was wearing a gray smock with rolled-up sleeves that left her olive arms bare. She was giv-

ing the midwife orders. "Rachida will choose the midwife,"
Boutros had said. She was fidgeting, Rachida. She stirred the
water in the washbasin. She said: "The cotton is on the upper
shelf to the right. Get some more alcohol." She opened the
linen cupboard. "Here are more sheets," she said.

It was also Rachida who, a short while ago, had said: "It
is a girl." Without turning toward me, she had shot these
four words at me over her shoulder.

But nothing could interfere with my joy. I had not yet seen
my daughter; nonetheless, I felt her presence. I gave myself
to my sensations. I was swaying in mid-air. Drops of fine rain
and long green leaves were caressing my body. My hair was
slightly damp at the roots. My forehead felt as soft as the
underside of a pigeon's wing. Tiny waves were running
through my arms and legs. And the smile on my face, I could
have traced it with my fingertips.

Rachida was taking off her gray smock and having trouble
with the buttons that ran down the back.She grumbled:
"How can I tell Boutros, poor man, that it is not a son?" Then
she came over to me and stood with her knees touching the
mattress. As she lowered her head to speak, her chin rested
on her chest and her harsh gaze fell upon me: "I am leaving
at once. I shall take the train home this very night. I could
not stand poor Boutros's disappointment very long. His un-
happiness! As it's only a girl, you don't need me."

My daughter, whom no one had shown me yet, was not far
away. I was no longer alone. It was as if I had been unbound.
All the knots had come loose. I was going to love and there
was now someone to love me all the time every hour of the
night or day.

Tears rose to my eyes. They made me beautiful. I was
beautiful, blooming, and I sang to myself silently, silently.

Without another word Rachida left. She did not even close
the door of my room after her, but I didn't listen to what she
was saying to her brother in the next room. Suddenly, I
heard the door open roughly, as if it were being torn from its
hinges.

"I am going out for a breath of fresh air," shouted Boutros,
and his steps were swallowed up in the stairwell.

*   *   *

Now I distinctly heard his footsteps and the sound of his cane. Bang! Bang! With all his might he was beating the bannister. The thuds echoed in my room.

My daughter was here. It was her cry I heard. Soon I would hold her against my body; the thought made me tremble with joy.

All the way down the staircase Boutros banged his cane furiously against the railing. He was tapping with rage. "A girl! A girl!" he must be muttering, I thought. The rough movements of his arms must make his shoulders shake. Rachida's rapid footsteps followed her brother's. She was probably wondering what she could do for him, the poor unfortunate one!

The stick came down on the railing, down on the wrought iron flowers. Every blow resounded in the bedroom with a deafening metallic crash. But these harsh sounds no longer reached me.

*   *   *

Part Three

With Mia I rediscovered my life.

My sadness dropped away like a dead skin. Physically, too, I was changing. My body was slimmer. I shook off the indifference which had turned it into an inert mass to be dragged about. Everything, even my smallest gesture, was alive. I felt the ground under my feet and the air on my cheeks. Mia's body against mine, Mia's arms around my knees, Mia's arms around my neck.

Even objects came to life. For Mia I found I had a magical tongue. Cups became boats surrounded by schools of enameled fish. Whole forests were hidden in the pleats of curtains, and the trees became flutes played upon by the wind. The carpets turned into mysterious cities where genies and fairies danced all night long. Destroyed by lightning, the tower of gilded bronze nonetheless remembered the name of each cloud.

I thought I was opening Mia's eyes, but I was opening my own as well.

Like the others, Om el Kher had been disappointed that I hadn't given birth to a son. At first, for fear of reviving my regrets, she did not even congratulate me. But I radiated so much joy that she could not help noticing.

To begin with, she asked after the child. Then one day she wanted to see her. No sooner had she come close than she discovered every possible virtue in the baby. She proclaimed:

"Girls! There's nothing like them! Not one of my sons has given me half the happiness Zeinab has. May Allah protect her, this child of my soul!"

She was laughing and rubbing her hands together; they made the sound of dry parchment. She shook her old wrinkled head from right to left, trying to make Mia smile. Om el Kher said: "She's going to smile! You'll see!" She made faces. She stuck out her gray tongue and made her eyes huge. She waved her arms about until her robe began to ripple in waves. Mia smiled. "Ah," sighed Om el Kher, "a child's smile brings such warmth!"

She ventured further, then, in her display of faces. In an effort to remember the songs of her childhood, she frowned. Scraps of old verses came to her memory, and she sang them, swaying on her feet, chanting:

> My hair can grow white
> And my hands wrinkle.
> My child has come
> With the sun on her lips.

Om el Kher's voice was hoarse and Mia sat up, hanging on to the railing of her bed, trying to hear better.

> The moon is her friend
> And the birds await her.
> My child has come
> My heart keeps me warm.

Om el Kher sang on and on. Happiness had entered the room.

Happiness! Was it finally a word I had a right to, me as well as others? I wanted to hold this word in my hands as if it were a fruit, to let endless mirrors reflect it so that everyone could have a share. But indifference is so strongly rooted that even happiness has trouble finding its way into people's hearts.

It was Om el Kher who taught Mia her first word:

"Let me try," she said, "I am experienced at it. Nine children and seventeen grandchildren!"

At first Mia was reticent. It seemed as if she wanted to preserve her liberty to exist outside the power of words. Om el Kher made her voice very soft and opened and closed her lips, coaxing Mia to enter the game. Her small body was tense and her eyes alert, but nothing came from her mouth except her breath.

Om el Kher came back each morning. She made Zeinab put the basket of vegetables under the kitchen table, then told her:

"Go on down. I'll join you later. I must see the child."

The day Mia pronounced her first word, Om el Kher turned to me: "You see! I am used to children." Her smile made wrinkles spread across her face. Mia dropped off to sleep right away.

This feeling of Mia asleep . . . .

I would get down on my knees to contemplate her. I brushed my lips against her arms, resting on the cool sheets. Her curls stood out in the dark, throwing shadows around her temples. Her nostrils quivered. Her mouth was half open. I rested my cheek against her palm and I felt her warm fingers tighten around my face.

The voice of Boutros said: "What are you doing? You are ridiculous! You'll wake the child!"

The voice of Boutros belonged to another world. When I was watching her sleep Mia never woke up.

* * *

More than three years passed before Mia and the blind man met for the first time in the path lined by eucalyptus trees. It was a short path which Mia and I often took to escape from the sun. We would walk from one end to the other in the shade thrown onto the ground by the trees' long gray leaves, forms as slender as the fingers of women. It amused Mia to chase these shadows when the breeze stirred them. One time she asked me to crush some eucalyptus leaves between my fingers so that she could smell their scent better.

It was a quiet path. Sometimes a woman carrying a jar on her head walked by, a peddler, or a man on a donkey, with a white parasol held above his head and, on his feet, clinging as if by a miracle, loose Turkish slippers.

I recognized the blind man because of his cane.

Mia was playing. She had found a flat black stone which she threw at the trees, then scampered to recover. The stone retrieved, she gave a shout of joy and ran back to show it to me. The blind man was moving the tip of his cane, walking toward us with a firm step. When he reached me, he stopped for a moment, raised his hand to his chest and said:

"Your child is growing. I can hear her running."

"She is four. Time goes by."

"I know. Time goes by. May Allah look over this child for you!"

I had not met the blind man since my first visit to the village years earlier, but when I opened my shutters or went for a walk, he was often there, moving about the countryside, his head held high, his cane barely grazing the ground. I would gaze after him. Often I had longed to talk to him because I thought he would understand me. But my shyness kept me from confiding in anyone. Others had to make the effort first. The blind man probably knew this. He also knew of my fondness for Ammal, and Ammal's secret, for he turned to me and said:

"You have shed light on Ammal. Her happiness is your doing."

Mia had come near us. She touched the man's robe and began to stroke his cane. She was not surprised by his empty eyes. "May Allah preserve you for your mother's sake! A child is like a second life."

Mia was still caressing his cane. She put the black stone in the blind man's hand, saying, "Throw it very far."

He bent forward and threw the stone low enough for it to bounce between the tree trunks. Mia caught my sleeve: "Look! Look!" she cried.

"May Allah preserve you for your mother's sake!" chanted the blind man. Then he left, wishing me a blessed day.

"Why are you leaving?" asked Mia.

"I have a long way to go. And I must walk slowly."

"Why?"

"I have many friends on the way, and if I walk too quickly, I don't have time to talk to them."

"Ah, yes." Mia handed me the stone, wanting me to take a turn at throwing it, but it was late. I bent down and picked her up. I held her in my arms and started running.

Her body is as warm as a quail's; her curls brush my lips. I run and she laughs: "Faster! Faster!" she cries.

The eucalyptus trees are far behind us. Mia trembles with joy. She turns her head to look at the cotton fields, and her hair covers part of my face. We spot the house. "Faster! Faster!" cries Mia.

How good it was! Perspiration ran down my temples. My legs felt light. Mia's weight in my arms gave me energy. I wanted time to stop so that my life would never advance beyond this moment.

That evening Boutros made fun of me. "You are ridiculous! You make a fool of yourself. You are no longer ten years old!"

I answered, "Yes. Yes," without hearing my own voice. I was distant, in another place. Again, I saw Mia as if she were still in my arms and I were still running. The road was unwinding before us and we could just catch the scent of the eucalyptus trees. Mia's body is curled against mine. Her nostrils quiver; her curls caress my cheek. She cries, "Faster! Faster!"

*   *   *

Ammal . . .

She came to see us sometimes during the afternoons when Boutros was out.

My father had sent me a phonograph and a few scratchy records. Mia and Ammal kissed, then they asked me to put on a record and to act out a story for them. The music was dreamy and it evoked a thousand images. I said, "Look! There is a house made of crystal at the end of the road. When the birds brush it with their wings, it rings like many tiny bells. Do you hear the bells? I am walking toward this house, walking toward the crystal house ... "

I told them also: "The path runs under my feet. It runs of its own accord. I don't have to make any effort to move, and yet I am moving. Behind each cotton plant there is a little girl. My skirt is wide, with leaves all around like a banana tree. The little girls catch hold of my skirt and the path carries them along too ... "

Ammal was sitting on the floor beside Mia and they were holding hands: "More! More!" they cried.

I acted out all the fantastic stories that came to mind, and I enjoyed them as much as the children did. I invented new gestures. I stretched out my fingers as if the things they tried to grasp were far away, out of reach. This was perhaps similar to what Ammal was trying to do with her clay.

"More! More!" cried the children.

I said, "Look! There is fruit falling everywhere. I don't know where it's coming from. I try to catch some of it in my arms, in my skirt. I call out to people to come. There is too much! There is enough for everybody. And so I call out. I shout with all my might. I shout, but nobody hears me! Nobody comes!"

I danced my story. Ammal and Mia brought it to life.

When I was finally tired, I sat down with them. Ammal reached into her bodice and brought out a small clay statue.

"It is for you," she said:. The figure represented a mother and her child. The bodies were blended together, and the child's face surged up from her mother's garments like a burgeoning sprout.

"My uncle Abou Mansour found the other statues," Ammal told me. "He says I am copying the works of Allah and I will be cursed." She went on to tell me how her uncle had thrown the figures on the ground and stamped on them. "They must be destroyed," he had shouted, "or you will bring bad luck to the village!" He had forbidden her to make any more.

"But I will make more," said Ammal, looking at me. She frowned with a determined air. "I will make more. Nobody can take away those I have in my head!"

Ammal would not give in. She was over twelve now and knew what she wanted. I felt the fire burning in her thin body. Ammal's gestures were also slow and patient. She had a turbulent heart and industrious hands, the sort of hands that build things.

I liked to watch Ammal. She was what I needed to be if I wanted to undermine the false walls hour after hour, without despondency, until they crumbled into the dark shadows they cast over us. I would love Ammal. That was all I could do, love her even more. Be part of the earth she needed in which to flourish.

Even Mia was fascinated when Ammal talked. I often hoped she would be more like Ammal than myself. They were happy together, Mia with her curls, Ammal in the yellow dress she always wore. The bodice reached up to her armpits now; she had added a band of green material at the bottom of the skirt to lengthen it.

When Ammal left, Mia ran after her as far as the landing, shouting "Goodbye!" Ammal went downstairs without turning around, and we could hear the light steady sound of her bare feet on the steps.

Soon after it was Boutros's heavy tread which climbed the stairs.

* * *

Happiness was so well established that it lent to everything a fragile and diluted air. Nothing but images of Mia shimmered before my eyes. And yet at night, when I had been thinking too much about Mia, her image played tricks on me and grew blurred and nearly impossible to evoke. Emotion seemed to come between her face and mine, and however often I spoke her name or recalled one of her gestures, the whole image refused to come to me.

I lived in this love in which I recreated myself. My family's indifference, Rachida's hatred, and Boutros's oppression no longer had any power over me. I dreamed also of another love, one that I would never experience. The connection be-

tween one love and the dream of another is natural. Love is
always powerful, whether it be the love of a man, of a child,
the love of others, or the love of creating something, which
Ammal possessed. Love is the response, the only response to
the anguish that seizes you when you are face to face with
yourself.

Inside my head there was no longer a stagnating pool.
Love for Mia had transformed me. And yet I never let myself
sink into happiness as if it were only a habit. When each day
dawned I told myself, "You are in a state of happiness."
When I heard Mia's voice and felt her arms around me, I told
myself: "This is happiness." And if Ammal worked next to
Mia with her clay, talking softly to her, I thought again:
"This is happiness." Every minute it was new. So different
from the treasures one hides in dark boxes, believing them
to be life insurance. I counted my happiness like the beads
of a rosary, turning it over and over in my hands.

At times this happiness frightened me. I felt a threat
hanging over it, and there were days when this fear invaded
me and pursued me even into my dreams.

I remember one of these dreams.

Mia and I were walking hand in hand. We came to a
clearing with trees growing in a circle around a very green
lawn. This green was much more vivid than any color I had
ever before seen. There was water and in the air a sweetness.
The reflections of this green light played on our bare arms
and the light was transparent as if mirrored from the surface of a lake. The trees were elongated; their leaves no
longer formed a compact mass but seemed to have dissolved
into a light rain stirred by a constant breeze. It seemed as if
invisible butterflies were caressing them with their wings.

Everything was still. I was not looking at Mia. To feel her
hand in mine was enough to reassure me that I was watching
over her.

And then I saw a man standing among the trees.

He was wearing a white flannel suit, clean and freshly
pressed, white shoes and a white tie. He was tall and slim,
as narrow as a candle. I did not see his face, at least I do not
remember seeing it. But his wavy hair was dark and shiny.
With a gesture of his long hand he beckoned to me to join

him. I do not know what there was about all the whiteness and the man's gleaming hair, but I felt sick. And though Mia's hand was still enclosed in mine, at the same time I saw her walking a few steps away. All of a sudden she came to the man and they held out their hands to each other. There was nothing I could do to hold her back. Their hands seemed to be calling to each other. With an air of sweetness Mia moved toward this man. I was helpless.

Mia went on walking. It seemed as if she were walking slightly above the ground. My hands and feet were like ice. I felt ill, terribly ill, and I couldn't move.

When their hands touched, they fell back together into the emptiness behind the curtain of trees . . .

* * *

Mia was six years old and she came to my waist. Boutros had finally given me permission to take her to town to buy her some clothes.

10 Abou Sliman took us to the station; the town was two hours away. In the compartment of the train Mia sat on my knee. I felt as if I were leaving behind an entire world. The train advanced with a deafening noise. The village, my room, Boutros's voice became memories. I imagined that I was setting out for a new life, as new as this youthfulness that Mia had restored to me, and I abandoned myself to my illusions.

I leaned nearer the window to see the tracks. I wanted the train to go faster, to leave everything familiar behind. I wanted it to cross whole continents and never to stop moving. Or if it must stop someplace, that it be in a country where memory did not exist.

But trains do not leave their tracks, and they do stop at stations. I stepped off the train onto the platform, and Mia jumped down into my arms.

We went off to explore the town. It was very much like the town of my childhood, only smaller. We walked past the shops and lingered in front of the windows. I felt free. I was holding my daughter by the hand. Boutros was far away. And suddenly his very existence seemed like a myth.

Our steps were light. We laughed, Mia and I, as we strolled along the sidewalks.

* * *

It was only a week later that Mia came down with a fever.
At first she agreed to stay in bed as if it were a new adventure. Her toys piled up on the blanket; the hairless bear, the
doll, the wooden construction game, and the tiny teacups
were scattered over the covers. Mia talked to her doll, saying, "We are going on a journey. My bed is a boat."

At the beginning I wasn't anxious. But at the end of a week
her fever was still high and I asked Boutros to call for the
doctor.

"It's nothing. It will pass." He pinched Mia's cheek, and
pronounced, "This child is not sick. Isn't that so, Mia? You
are not sick, are you?"

Mia smiled. "No, I am not sick."

She asked me a thousand questions, begging me to tell her
new stories. Whenever she heard Abou Sliman's steps, she
called his name: "Abou Sliman!" until he came and then she
held out her small hand, smiling.

A little later I became worried again. I noticed that Mia
had not changed her doll's dress for two days. The child did
not seem to suffer and yet at night she moaned softly. The
fever never left her. I saw shadows settle under her eyes, and
there was a perpetual dampness in the hollow of her palms.

"It's that trip to town," Boutros said. "She's not used to
town air." He added that I never thought of anyone but
myself. "Here is the result!" he said.

This time I insisted: "Bring the doctor, Boutros. This has
lasted too long!"

"All right. I'll phone him." To himself he muttered something about never being able to rest in peace. Before leaving
the room he leaned over Mia: "Well, no smile for your father?"

I insisted: "You must call the doctor, Boutros. Today!"

But he left without answering.

I stood still for a moment, then at the thought that Boutros
might forget, I started running. I crossed the two rooms and
the entrance hall and leaned over the banister, shouting:
"Boutros, the doctor must come today! Today!" I repeated.

Boutros didn't answer. I heard his footsteps on the stairs. The office door opened and then closed behind him.

I returned to Mia's room, stopping short at the threshold, struck by the sight of the bed. It seemed larger than usual, and Mia's face seemed lost among the sheets. The room was dark for the shutters were closed. A weak ray of light fell on the toys piled up on the blue quilt at the foot of the bed. It resembled a mound. The image took root deeply in my mind. I couldn't distinguish one toy from another. They formed a solid mass which stood out in the dark. A mound. I was unable to take a step forward. The toys looked like a heap of stones. They frightened me. Above them, the luminous light formed a triangle in which the dust was whirling, throwing a transparent gray light on the mound.

Anxiety kept me rooted to the spot; it would have been better if I had done something to dissolve it, touch the toys, fix Mia's head on the pillows, anything. I was certain of only one thing: if the doctor did not come right away, it would be too late. I must remind Boutros. Shout if necessary. Again, I ran through the two rooms and the hall. I dashed down the stairs with the sentence on the tip of my tongue: "The doctor must come at once!"

When I reached the office I turned the doorknob roughly and darted past the clerks, unconcerned by their amazement. Boutros's door was ajar. He was seated at his desk searching through a drawer of papers.

From the threshold I started shouting: "At once, Boutros! We need a doctor at once!"

"But I have just gotten here. Give me time."

I shouted louder still. Behind me I could hears chairs scraping. The door was open and the employees were talking:

"The little girl is ill?"

"Children often have fevers. It's the beginning of the hot weather."

"Mothers always worry."

Boutros clapped his hands until someone appeared: "Close the door," he ordered, "and have someone bring us two very cold glasses of mulberry juice."

When the clerk had left, Boutros added: "An iced drink, that will calm you."

But it didn't calm me. I stood with arms extended, my hands planted on his desk. Leaning forward, bringing my face close to his, I cried out: "We need a doctor!"

Slowly, Boutros picked up the receiver. Then he put it down again and unraveled the telephone wires. "I'll have these shortened; they are too long. Sit down now. Sit down." He spoke to me as if he were humoring a woman who had gone mad.

Abou Sliman entered with two glasses of iced fruit drink on a tray. I refused mine. Boutros shrugged and signaled to the servant to set down the tray and leave the room. Again he picked up the receiver while taking small sips of his drink. There were green ink stains on the leather of the desk top, and the gilt border was peeling. I remained standing while Boutros asked for the doctor's number. My frustration brought tears to my eyes. Every minute lost seemed irretrievable. All of a sudden there was a voice on the other end of the line, but before Boutros had time to say a word, I snatched the phone out of his hands.

"You are mad!" He pushed me aside. Now he was speaking. Someone told him that the doctor was out visiting his patients and would not be back until evening. "All right then. Tell him to come this evening." When he was through, he turned to me: "Calm down, or I shall have to call for Rachida. She'll come at once if I write to her. I can count on Rachida. But I think we have taken advantage of her quite enough up to now."

The thought of Rachida taking care of my child chilled me to the bone. I had to calm myself. "No, no, I am all right now, Boutros. You must understand, I was very frightened. I am better now." I told him that I would return to Mia's bedside. "I am calm now. I'll see you later on."

In the adjoining room I passed between the rows of tables at which the clerks worked. They made a show of getting up as I came through. Brahim, who had a wart at the corner of one eye, accompanied me to the staircase:

"Children often have fevers," he said. "It is the beginning of the hot weather."

In her room I found Mia sleeping. Her breathing was regular. One by one I removed the toys that had terrified me so. In isolation, separated from one another, they seemed noth-

ing more than toys. A wooden cube, a hairless doll, a little
house with green shutters. I put them away in the bottom of
the armoire. I had been anxious over nothing. Toys were
only toys and children everywhere became ill and got better
again. I was calm, but I had to wait until the next day for the
doctor's visit.

The night revived my phantoms. I was sitting in a chair
that I had drawn up to Mia's bed. Our hands were linked
together on the blue quilt. Boutros was sleeping in the next
room. I could hear him snoring.

The hours dragged on. I had put the lamp on the floor so
the light wouldn't awaken Mia. In this dim light I could
watch her face. I forced myself to believe that unfailing
attention could avert disaster, and when sleep finally overwhelmed me, I awoke with a start, filled with remorse. It
seemed to me that a fatal presence was in the room and that
a battle had begun between us. Awake, I felt strong. I held
Mia's hand; I took her pulse; she was breathing with difficulty, but I was relieved that she was sleeping, leaving me
to fight this battle alone. I put all my strength into my gaze,
trying to protect her.

At six when Mia woke up, I had the feeling that I had
saved her from the night.

                              *   *   *

The doctor did not arrive until late in the morning. After
examining the child, he diagnosed a severe case of typhoid.
Then he sat down, took out a prescription form from his
black leather case, and started searching his pockets for his
pen. "I must have forgotten it," he said.

I went into the livingroom to bring a pen and I told Abou
Sliman to warn Boutros that the doctor would be leaving
soon. Mia was crying because I had been away for a minute.
She could not bear to be without me now, and whenever I
went near the door her eyes called me back. I handed the pen
to the doctor who sat, legs crossed, playing with the zipper
of his leather case. As he wrote out the prescription, he
repeated that it was a severe case of typhoid; he said that he
should have been called much earlier. Now I must comply

with everything he had written down, follow everything to
the letter.

I tried to banish my fears. I told myself, "With good care
and medicine, she will recover." The doctor was not listening. He nodded mechanically, but his gaze was fixed on the
drapes as if he were trying to guess what sort of fabric they
were made of.

As soon as he was gone I ordered the medicine and I ap-
plied myself to nursing Mia. On a cardboard sheet I wrote
down her temperature with a red pencil. I made my motions
concentrated and precise. I covered all the tables with white
cloths. I dressed myself in white as if, thanks to these conventions, I could conjure away Mia's illness.

Mia was now indifferent to her toys. She accepted my
constant care with a resignation that was beyond her years.
I tried to tell her stories but I had trouble finding the words.
It was even more difficult for me to discover images. Mia
turned her head away and repeated: "No, no . . ." Even the
sound of my voice exhausted her.

The doctor came back regularly. One day he said he would
bring a colleague for consultation. I was afraid my nerves
would snap, especially at night with the weight of the darkness and the day as well upon my shoulders. My fears in-
creased. At times I would jump up from my chair and stand
over Mia, scrutinizing her face. I would put my cheek to her
mouth to feel her burning breath. I waited for morning to
come and banish my fears. But at the same time I was afraid
that the morning might bring me closer to something far
more terrifying.

Those days passed too, those days too.

I don't remember anything. Mia was everything. I knew
nothing else. I don't know whether the doctor returned. I
don't know whether Boutros was often beside the bed. I
seemed to hear, but through a mist or a fog, the voice of Om
el Kher: "My soul is with you," said the voice. From the
corner of the livingroom came muffled tears, perhaps those
of Ammal. And one day, I think, Abou Sliman brought me
a wicker basket for Mia; the blind man had given it to him.
I scarcely remember all of this. I remember nothing else
actually. And yet the days were endless.

On the morning of my true death, Mia looked up at me, and she was smiling on that morning.

I leaned over to receive the smile in the corners of her lips, when she left me forever.

*   *   *

The women of the village are at the bottom of the staircase. They are huddled together, a motionless black mass. At first they wailed loudly, expressing their mourning, and their cries were like the strange cries of the wood owl. But for the past two days they have been silent. They just sit on the four bottom steps, all of them at the bottom. If someone wishes to pass, they shrink back into themselves to make way. For two days they have been silent. They don't even know if I am aware that they are there, and yet they remain at the bottom of the stairs. Om el Kher, Zeinab, Ratiba, and the others who have spent the night there. They brought some dry bread to sustain them. They keep it near their breasts under their robes. In the daytime they sit with their chins in their hands. At night they sleep on the stairs.

A large silent mass of black at the bottom of the staircase, the women watch over my sorrow.

And I, upstairs in Mia's room. Seated on a chair. One of my arms dangling over the back. Nobody has been able to make me move. Voices reach me from the livingroom where Boutros is receiving condolences.

"It is the will of God," say the sisters. They have spent two nights watching over the dead child.

"What have I done to offend heaven?" moans Boutros. "I am a righteous man!"

"You must rest," say the clerks. "It does no good to waste one's strength."

"She was an angel," say the nuns. "God chose her for himself."

"I too," says a woman. "I too have lost a child. But God has blessed me ever since."

At the bottom of the stairs Om el Kher is silent. And Zeinab is silent. And Ammal, and the others are all silent.

Now and again Abou Sliman leans over the banister to take part in the women's silence.

"What have I done to offend heaven?" repeats Boutros. "I am a righteous man!" and he weeps noisily.

"You are a Christian," say the sisters. "The will of God must be done."

"My son also had typhoid," says a voice. "I nearly lost him."

"One needs a lot of courage," someone tells Boutros. "You'll need all your strength."

I thrust this noise away from my ears. I repeat: "My life, my young life ..." I repeat: "Where are you, my life, my young life?" I no longer know what I am saying.

I am alone in this room which Mia has left. It seems huge all of a sudden, this room. The legs of my chair throw slender shadows on the floor. Still, the voices are all around me. People say they want to see me. I say "No." The voices are still there. They evoke memories. Each one has known some illness. Each one has known death. Boutros explains that city air is bad for children. And the voices approve of what he says. Do I really hear all this? I am so far away ...

And yet I am not alone.

At the bottom of the staircase are these women who watch over my suffering. They have not uttered a word for two days.

*　*　*

I no longer wanted to live.

Was this life, these days which followed one another without meaning? Now I suffered from something much deeper than boredom. Sleep no longer had the power to soothe me.

11 Boutros wore a black band around his sleeve. When I tried to speak of Mia, he turned away nervously, as if he wanted to shield himself from painful memories.

I tried to recall my moments of happiness, to hold onto them, and at the same time I felt a kind of fear, as if still another danger hovered around Mia, one that was somehow my fault. Nothing calmed the cry of pain that reverberated within me. Days came one after another, smothering the past, but they brought no relief. My pain never stopped burning.

I wanted to put an end to it. I knew where the river was deepest. It was harvest time and Boutros came home late.

Finally, one afternoon I left the house. I walked along the road, the road that runs beside the river, leading to the town. At first the dust rose under my feet and the sky was lit up by fiery patches. I did not want to think of anything or of anybody. I put the thought of Om el Kher and her sorrow out of my mind. I rejected Ammal, whom I was betraying. I was going to meet my death. The closer I got to it, the more familiar it seemed, this death I hated so much. The death of my mother, so early, this unfair death, the death of my mother. The death of Mia, a violation of her youth, and the death of the man whom I had seen flaming like a torch in the city streets. So many deaths! Yes, now everything seemed, suddenly, simple and easy. I was almost exultant. I repeated "Ammal! Ammal!" as if I wanted to give her my last breath to add to her strength. I wanted Ammal to fulfill her own life.

When the sun goes down and the asphalt pavement cools, it no longer sticks to the soles of the feet. Each of my footsteps rang out distinctly. I walked in the middle of the road without meeting any cars. Under the metal bridge farther on, to my left, the water was deepest.

I walked more and more quickly. My temples were throbbing. I ran down the road quickly, as if I were going to meet all the roads on earth. I heard my heels clicking against the asphalt. The bridge was tinted with the colors of the setting sun. I heard my heels clacking on the asphalt, as if they were heels, simply heels that belonged to nobody, heels that pursued me with their clacking. There was a rustling sound in my head. Death, perhaps it were only this, a sweet rustling sound, like the one going around and around in my head, a sound to which one had only to abandon herself in order to die.

I ran over the bridge, stopping where the water was deepest, yellowish, with large waves that destroyed themselves and then were reborn. I leaned over the parapet to see the water better.

I don't know how long I remained there, staring at the water.

* * *

Night had fallen when I found myself again on the path that led to the house.

Here again was the asphalt road, the dusty path, the village, the avenue of banana trees, and the landlord's white house. Here too are the stairs, the entrance hall, the velvet draperies which I draw back and here, too, the voice of Boutros:

"Is this the proper time to come home? Where have you been? Answer me. Where have you been?"

"I went for a walk. I walked very far and I forgot the time."

"Don't let it happen again. Abou Sliman has had to heat the dinner twice."

He waved his arm toward the kitchen. The black band was shabby now, having lost its sheen. "I bought you a watch. There is no excuse for being late. And what is the reason for roaming around the streets? I have already told you, I don't like you to be out of the house after five. Do you hear?"

"Yes, Boutros," I answered, but I was thinking of the river. It was dark, somber and grave, this water; it could carry you very far away, it made no difference where, toward God, toward oblivion, toward who knows what encounter!

"The rice is dry, and it's your fault," Boutros said. "I've never eaten such bad rice."

The river flowed on past towns and fields, taking my body with it. The river took me flowing along between its banks where women walked carrying jars and bundles on their heads. Now and then a gray donkey trotted along by itself. The weeping willow trees waste a lifetime watching their reflections in the water. The river sweeps one along under the bridges, and you discover the undersides of boats. Your death and the rivers will soon flow together into the bottom of the sea.

"Om el Kher has brought three jars of honey," said Boutros. "You will serve me this honey every morning with fresh cream."

The river didn't want me, didn't want the dead person I could have become. It was waiting for no one, it flowed on. For the river to carry you away you must run after it; otherwise, the river will abandon you on its steep bank. It will leave you to your own death, your small death, dry and solitary.

*　　*　　*

Between my pain and the shame I felt at not ever having accomplished anything, I was slowly poisoning myself. Every one of the people around me seemed heavy with symbolic meaning, and in my eyes took on exaggerated importance.

The image of Boutros, for example, went far beyond Boutros. He had become the bogeyman of children's dreams. I loaded upon him my own sorrows as well as those of the whole world. Boutros was ugly and unlovable. He killed all vital impulses and, praying through pursed lips, he invaded others with his calculating mind. His voice and his massive body came between me and other people, between me and life itself, crushing the slightest joy. Boutros was my interment, and my fear of him struck me dumb.

Boutros's image was blown up, becoming confused with the image of my father, who had never known how to extend himself except to himself, becoming confused, as well, with the images of my brothers who respected nothing but money. Poverty was everywhere. Boutros showed only indifference toward it. To me, he had become the symbol of those who live by principles as dried up as their souls. At this thought above all others, I hated him even more than before.

I was alone. My reason to live had been snatched away from me. I stood before a wall which either rejected or deformed my own voice. You must understand. I was scarcely thirty, and what could I possibly hope for? Before me was a horizon filled with obstructions. Others besides myself must have felt their souls worn away by the interminable length of a life without love. They will understand me. If I cry out, I am crying out for them as well as myself. It is also for them that I weep. And if there is only one who understands me, it is for her that I protest from the depths of my being as loudly as I can.

But soon it will be too late even for cries. Everything will be useless. Soon there will be nothing to do but to make an empty space around myself and burrow down inside of it.

*   *   *

I started by keeping Om el Kher away. Images of Mia seemed stuck to her, floating in the folds of her black robes. I couldn't bear this any longer. Om el Kher came to see me faithfully, but I avoided her.

For the same reason I avoided Ammal. I could do nothing more for her. I wanted nothing but emptiness and silence. I refused everything, even the memory of Mia. I refused this too.

Often, before going to sleep, I felt Mia next to me. Her arms around my neck, her feet nestling between my legs. I turned over beneath the sheets, buried my head in the pillow and repeated: "No, no, I don't want this!" The memory of Mia was tenacious. One night I saw her face pressed against the window pane looking in at me. Quickly, I got up and drew the curtains. Outside on the path, washed white by the moon, the blind man was walking. I recognized him by his pale turban. I wanted him to go away too! I was standing at the window. Mia was no longer there. But suddenly I saw her riding on the blind man's right shoulder. Their backs were turned toward me and they were moving away together. Go away, both of you! I pulled the curtains closed so I could remain in the dark.

The next day I was no longer able to move from my bed. My legs were completely immobile. I had driven all the life out of them.

                              *   *   *

Boutros was striking his forehead with his fist. "What will become of me?" he repeated over and over again. "What will become of me?"

At first he tried to persuade me that there was nothing wrong. He threw back the bedclothes. "Walk!" he commanded. But my legs refused to obey.

"What will become of me?" wailed Boutros.

And then he began to abuse me, complaining about all he had put up with because of me. Once again, he accused me of being responsible for Mia's death. "It's because of that trip to town! That's where she caught the disease!"

When the doctor came Boutros inquired whether my condition was contagious.

"No," replied the doctor, "but she will not be able to move. For quite a long time she won't be able to see to the household work. However, at her age, this should pass."

Boutros sank heavily into an armchair, his hands dangling from his wrists. "What a tragedy this is for me!" he repeated.

The doctor was seated at the foot of my bed. He took the prescription pad out of his leather satchel and removed his pen from his pocket.

"I have not forgotten it this time," he said to me.

He wrote slowly, adding an illegible signature at the bottom of the sheet.

"You won't be able to move for a long time," he told me. Then, turning to Boutros, he went on: "Misfortunes come all at one time! It's only four months, isn't it?"

"Six months," replied Boutros with a sigh.

Slowly, the doctor shook his head. Then he got up, walked over to Boutros and put his hand on his shoulder: "Courage," he said. "That's how it is. Misfortunes come all at one time!"

Abou Sliman appeared, carrying a black lacquered tray which held three glasses of water and three cups of coffee. The doctor sat down again in the armchair next to Boutros. They drank their coffee. I had refused mine. I lay back and watched the two men.

I would never again move. What was more, I did not want to move. If only I could have banished the thoughts that ran around in my head! Endlessly, I told myself that I had been born for something else. Repeatedly, I told myself that only some sort of action could set me free. But I had been incapable of any kind of action.

* * *

Boutros was not long in calling for Rachida. He wrote the letter on the round table in the livingroom, and I caught sight of him through the half-open door, searching for his words. And Rachida was not long in answering. Tears came to his eyes when Boutros read her reply: "I feel as if a heavy load has been lifted from my shoulders," he said.

Boutros came home only at meal times, and Abou Sliman soon got used to settling me in the high-backed armchair and pushing it into the livingroom. I stayed there all day without

demanding anything except that the shutters remain closed.
The semi-darkness put to sleep the anxiety aroused in me by
the sight of objects, allowing me to close my eyes for a time
and to forget.

The day of Rachida's arrival Boutros did not conceal his
impatience. As soon as lunch was finished, he and Abou
Sliman left to meet her at the station.

It was winter and night fell quickly. I lit the lamp that
stood on a table next to my chair. I knew that I must savor
these few remaining moments of solitude, for soon Rachida
would be here, and then her footsteps would be everywhere.

I saw, first of all, a shadow. I must have dozed off, for I had
heard no noise. The shadow spread across the carpet and
collided with the wall. It was thin, a thin shadow with a face
in tears. Then I felt Rachida's lips on my forehead.

"And now what has happened to my poor Boutros?" she
murmured.

Rachida settled down in the house; rather, she took up
once again the place that had always been hers. I soon realized that every object here awaited her. There is something
that lingers around objects which belong to those who chose
them in the first place, something impalpable that never
wears off. Near the artificial flowers, the dark furniture
loaded with knickknacks and the thick draperies, Rachida
was at home. It was she who had chosen the gray shade of
the walls and the imitation marble frieze that ran around
the baseboard.

When Rachida gave Abou Sliman orders, her tone was
cutting:

"Go and get my suitcase. Don't dawdle! You know I don't
like to wait!"

While Abou Sliman dragged his tired feet up and down the
stairs, Rachida came and went in the house. She took off her
shoes and put on a pair of blue felt slippers that she had
pulled out of a large bag. She paid no attention to me. She
seemed suddenly to feel much younger, as if the past sixteen
years had not occurred at all, for she was once again sharing
her brother's life. She hurried from one room to another,
examining each piece of furniture. Now she was opening my
armoire:

"I'm putting your dresses away," she said. "In your present state, what good are they? They'll be better off in my suitcase."

She started taking my dresses off their hangers and throwing them on top of one another. Abou Sliman returned, carrying in one hand a heavy suitcase bound by leather straps and in the other, a smaller one tied with rope. On his back he bore a huge green cloth bag. He moved painfully.

"Here you are at last!" exclaimed Rachida when she caught sight of him in the doorway.

She was taking out my coat and my woolens. "All this must be put away somewhere." My clothing lay about on the chairs and the tables. Some things had slipped to the floor. "The armoire must be cleaned," Rachida went on. "Abou Sliman, go and bring me cleaning supplies."

Off went Abou Sliman, soon returning with a bowl of soapy water and a brush. Rachida unpacked her things. The house was a mess.

Rachida made herself entirely at home. She granted me no more importance than one would give to a cumbersome object that was in the way.

Two years went by this way, or so I believe.

*   *   *

At the beginning of my illness Ammal continued to bring her uncle's cheese to me. When she looked at me her eyes filled with tears. Rachida soon forbade her to come into the livingroom. She did not like Ammal and she claimed that I made a spectacle of myself.

The last time I saw Ammal I gathered enough strength to talk about her clay figures, and she promised me she would never give up making them. "I promise you!" she exclaimed with sudden passion. The last glimmer of will I possessed was directed toward her. I told myself that if only Ammal were saved, my life would not have been entirely meaningless.

Days and still more days passed in the semi-darkness behind the closed shutters.

Sometimes I heard Om el Kher's voice in the kitchen. She asked after me but she was told that visits tired me. And then again Rachida's footsteps, Rachida's complaints, Rachida's shadow on the walls that imprisoned me.

My presence no longer bothered Boutros and Rachida. They talked about me as if I were not there. When she got up, Rachida never said "Good morning." But Boutros never forgot to place a kiss on my forehead each evening, a ritual he could not do without. Soon every single thought of my entire day would become concentrated on the moment when I would inevitably feel the contact of his lips with my skin.

This thought stirred in me a last impulse toward revolt. The door would open and I would wait, rigid, for the brown lips to touch my forehead. One day I would no longer be able to bear it. I knew this.

But what am I saying? What have I just said? Everything is confused. There is an unceasing noise in my head. Everything is confused. And that other noise? What is it?

I seem to hear my name called out, and someone is crying out Boutros's name. Voices, they are coming closer and closer. What has happened?

Steps on the staircase, many steps, crowding. Whose are they? I don't know. I don't want to know. I am afraid of nothing now. Let them come, with their noisy steps and their shouts! Let them invade the room, all of them!

I am dead to this story, and everything within me is silent.

* * *

In the entrance where the velvet drapes have been torn down by the crowd, Ammal stands on tiptoe trying to catch a glimpse of Samya.

12 Hussein, the first to go in, sees everything in spite of his weak eyes. Shouts clash like sticks knocking together. Rachida speaks loudly. Barsoum feels the heat climbing in his arms:

"Throw her out of that chair! Kill her!" he shouts.

Women beat their breasts with their open palms and wail like wood owls.

Om el Kher thrusts her hand in her mouth to keep back her tears. She wants to forget. She does not want to look at Samya, nor the dead man.

Maybe they will kill the woman right here?

Farid comes near, the skin of his face yellow, tight.

"We will trample you!" he screams. Big drops of sweat roll off his temples.

But Samya is far away. She doesn't even seem to be breathing. Only the way she holds herself, her breasts raised, her hands on the arms of her chair, elbows slightly lifted as though she were about to stand up, gives the impression that she is still alive. Ammal sees her, but from the side. She cannot tear away her eyes.

"You will be saved, Ammal!" Had this lifeless face ever expressed those words? It is so white now, this face of Samya's, white as a stone. Ammal hears the unspoken words. Ammal feels so many things that she yearns to shout them out all at the same time. But what words would she use?

Rachida finds words. As the days pass, she will tell it all!
As she speaks, her eyebrows meet and two furrows pull her
mouth down on either side of her lower lip. Her voice grates
like a file scraping bronze. People circle around Rachida.
People are crying out with her.

But the sudden arrival of the chief of police hushes the
voices, and the crowd makes way for the officials. There is
the heavy tread of the policemen on the steps. They are
coming to get the woman, to take her away in the police van
that is waiting in the street.

The Maamour wants to hurry things along; he wants to get
home in time for his evening meal. A month ago he married
Fatma, a girl of fourteen, as beautiful as a fruit. Fatma! The
Maamour sees her as if she were there, wearing the green
dress he chose for her, sitting with her hands on her thighs.
When he enters the room she gets up to leave the only armchair to him.

The Maamour clears the crowd out of the room. Only the
four men remain who will carry the armchair down the
stairs. They bend down together and lift the chair, but the
woman doesn't move. She seems to have so little part in all
this that the Maamour has not even thought about questioning her.

The men carry the chair through the entrance hall. For a
second Ammal is tempted to cry out: "I am here!" But Samya
would not hear her. And what if she were to hurl herself
against the crowd, all by herself and to snatch Samya away!
But what would she do then with this Samya of stone?

The four men have difficulty moving the chair down the
stairs. One of the policemen goes first. At each step he turns
around to say, "More to the right," or, "a little to the left."

No one remains in the stairwell now except Fakhia with
the pock-marked face. Her chin resting on the railing, she
watches through the eyes of a screech owl.

"They are bringing down the murderess!" she cries.

And they all rush up the steps with raised fists. The policemen wave their sticks to threaten the crowd.

"Throw her out of that chair! Trample her!" shouts the
crowd.

The woman doesn't hear anything. She no longer sees anything, not even the blind man who manages to hold his own in the crowd, his head held so high that his white turban towers above the heads of the others.

"Throw her to the ground. She has the devil in her!"

The blind man clenches his fist. He feels the ground give way under the tip of his cane. He pounds the ground harder and harder. He wants to beat his silent rage into the earth so deeply that she will never forget it.

*   *   *

There is no one but Ammal left in the house.

She knows that she must go away from this place. When your fingers can give birth to creatures who are closer to life than the living will ever be, you are not alone. She must go away, far away from the suffocation and the decay that come from fear.

Ammal walks to the staircase and looks down. She raises her dress a little above her knees, holding it with both hands.

Waiting a second to catch her breath, she begins to run. Ammal runs.

"It is Ammal. She is running!" cries Fakhia.

"She is frightened."

At this cry the blind man stops beating the ground with his cane.

"Ammal is running!"

Leaning against the wall, the blind man breathes in peace. How she can run, Ammal! How she runs!

*   *   *